THE CLONE CODES

PATRICIA C. MCKISSACK

FREDRICK L. MCKISSACK

JOHN MCKISSACK

THE CLONE

CODES

SCHOLASTIC PRESS
NEW YORK

Library of Congress Cataloging-in-Publication
data available.
2009024076
ISBN: 978-0-439-92983-7

10 9 8 7 6 5 4 3 2 1   10 11 12 13 14

Printed in the United States of America   23

First edition, February 2010
Book design by Phil Falco

To John, James Everett, Peter, and Mark

THE CLONE CODES

■ All clones are to be identified by number or alphanumerical designation. The use of names is restricted.

■ Clones have no rights under a court of law and are recognized solely as property.

■ Groups of clones in excess of three are not permitted without direct human supervision.

■ Attempting to educate a clone beyond its work model specifications is forbidden and punishable in accordance with article 3C74.

■ The manufacture of a clone in the likeness of a child is a capital offense.

❚ Imprinting the ability to mimic human emotions into a clone's behavioral patterns is forbidden.

❚ A clone that disobeys a direct order must immediately be taken to a processing center for decommissioning.

❚ Instructing a clone to lie is restricted.

❚ Since clones are not citizens, they may not participate in elections.

Issued by the Clone Humane Society, the government agency for the protection and processing of clones

//MyStory/Leanna/Personal
Real Date: Wednesday, September 19, 2170
Real Time: 2:00:00 pm
Virtual Date: September 18, 1859
Virtual Time: Midnight
Subject: Escape

I lean back in my chair and open my virtual program with the usual command: "All-Virtual School #32445, student ID 122-243-9080."

Instantly, I arrive on a plantation. In the distance, I hear the first notes of a spiritual floating on the night wind. I know this song.

"Steal away. Steal away.

Steal away home."

It's used as a signal from the conductor leading the runaways to freedom. I listen as a mother says her good-byes.

"No time to waste, son — go!"

"I'll be back for you soon as I can," the boy tells her.

"You being free is good enough," she says as they hug each other.

Quietly, we slip out of the quarters, through the grass and toward the large live oak on the far side of the fields.

Men and women of all ages join us. A man with two small children arrives last, which brings our number to eleven. Just then, a woman steps from the shadows and stands in the moonlight. I've read three books written about this powerful person — it's Harriet Tubman! I'm honored to be in the presence of the most famous conductor on the Underground Railroad. So what if this is virtual — it feels so *real*. The smells of early autumn and the sounds of night creatures are all around me. What a cool way to learn history.

Harriet tells us, "Chir'ren, aine gon' be no turnin' 'round once we be on our way. We goin' all the way to freedom or he'ven. Y'all hear me?" We nod our heads.

"We're freedom bound. Let's get goin'."

Harriet is firm as she leads us into the woods. The Moon and stars are our guides. "See that bright light there?" she says, pointing. "That's the North Star. Follow it and it'll lead you to freedom."

We run through thorny bushes that rip my bare feet and ankles. Low-hanging tree branches grab my hair and scratch my face. My clothes are torn. I stumble over rocks and struggle to keep up.

This virtual adventure goes from fun to painful, then to scary when I hear hounds in the distance. It's much easier to *read* about escaping from slavery than it is to actually *do* it.

The others hear the hounds, too. Harriet tells us not to panic. "Trust me. I know what to do," she says. "Just keep runnin'!"

I hesitate, thinking maybe I should return to our virtual homeroom and wait for the other students to complete their programs. But I don't want to go back and look like a wimp.

While I wrestle with my own fear, I feel a tug at my pant leg. A little kid named Dodger, who had been running in front of me earlier, trips over a rock and falls hard. "Help," he pleads. I wipe a trickle of blood from his eyebrow.

Since I'm in virtual, it's easy for me to go back to safety. But what choice does Dodger have?

"Move when I say *move*," Harriet snaps.

I grab Dodger's hand, yank him up, and we keep running. "Can't stop," I whisper. Dodger holds my hand tightly.

Harriet confuses the dogs by putting red pepper in our tracks. We zigzag our way downriver and cross in the shallows. That's where the hounds lose our scent and turn back, but we keep following the North Star.

When she's sure no more hounds are on our heels, Harriet lets us rest. We give thanks and hold one another in silent expressions of joy.

"Don't get too excited," Harriet warns. "Defeatin' the dogs is jus' one small victory. We got to make it all the way into Canada. So take a swallow of water and let's be on our way."

Now Harriet leads us through swampy lowlands. The canopy of trees blocks the Moon. To stay on course, Harriet looks for moss that grows on the north side of trees. Mosquitoes and leeches make every step dreadful. We swat and claw at our skin. Still, we stumble and crawl forward.

By virtual morning, we've made it through the swamp to a farmhouse that sits in a clearing. I have never been so glad to see a house in my life.

Harriet gives a birdcall. A minute later, we hear the

response. I'm too tired to talk, but I hold on to Dodger, whose body is hot and limp.

Quietly and quickly, the owner of the farmhouse leads us to the attic, where he hides us behind a false wall. Now I understand why slave hunters got so frustrated when the slaves they were chasing seemed to vanish as if on an underground railroad.

The farmer's wife brings us food, and we eat in silence. The plain bread, dried fruit, and water taste so good. For the moment, our group is safe.

"You done a'right tonight," Harriet tells us. "We gon' be here 'til night come again, so rest."

When Dodger falls asleep, the virtual program ends. I am the last to return to the homeroom at All-Virtual School.

I rub my eyes and stretch. I can still smell the night and the hay that was our bedding in that farm's hidden place.

Our teacher, Ms. Jamison, asks the class, "What did you learn from your experiences?"

Jared Stringwood is the first to speak. "I was a slave owner in my program. I owned three slaves — not three hundred like on some plantations." Jared is quiet for a moment, like he's thinking. "One of my slaves was a blacksmith, and I sold him for a huge profit."

"How did that make you feel?" Ms. Jamison asks.

Jared answers with uncertainty. "Confused. Angry. Sad. How can one *person* so easily sell another *person*?"

"That is a question that still lingers," Ms. Jamison says.

My friend Sandra speaks next. "I was an abolitionist who

spoke at a church in Ohio against slavery and for women's rights. I even met Sojourner Truth."

I speak up next. "I was a runaway slave on the run with Harriet Tubman."

"A great woman," Ms. Jamison says. "In all her trips leading slaves out of the South, she never lost a fugitive."

A smile rises up in me, knowing Dodger has made it safely to Canada. I lean back in my chair, tired and happy.

Ms. Jamison gives us our next virtual assignment. "Tomorrow we will go to the first Lincoln-Douglas debate, then to the Battle of Gettysburg later on this week."

Class is over.

"Save virtual program 1859: #32445 and exit." I disengage my commglasses, wipe my eyes, and stretch. My back hurts. My neck is stiff. Even though I've been running through fields and swamps during class, I actually haven't moved out of the chair in my bedroom for hours. That's what I love about being a student at a virtual school. I go to class without ever leaving home.

Being part of the All-Virtual School (AVS), the first of its kind in Missouri, has turned out to be totally frisk. Mom says I'm lucky to have been chosen for the pilot class. I wasn't so sure about that at first. I thought I'd miss going to a school building every day and fringing — that's hanging out with my friends — but now I'm sold on AVS.

The best part of AVS is the commglasses that link me to the Universe. I never go anywhere without them because who wants to be disconnected? Besides, I'm always in need of my computer, telephone, data storage, camera, T screen, video recorder, and virtual portal, which are all programmed into the glasses.

The AVS and commglasses are a new way of learning. How many kids can get history by *living* it and never leaving home? The same is true for PE. Some kids still get together in a gym to exercise. Not me. I go through my whole school day in virtual mode. I still gotta work hard, though. And as far as PE goes, virtual doesn't make it any easier.

My school day isn't over until I've done a sixty-minute work-out. Ten minutes into my routine, my commglasses ring. I answer. "Telephone. Hey!"

It's Sandra, whose hologram appears in my bedroom.

"I just walked a half mile and I need a break," she says, collapsing on the bed. Sandra hates exercising. She'd rather talk than run.

I laugh. "Okay, San, but only for a minute, then back to work! All A's with a failing heart rate could stop you from getting into a top-ranked university. Can't let that happen." I never stop pedaling my V-bike.

"Okay, Miss Likely to Succeed." Sandra's breathing hard.

"Look, if I'm going to make the swifting team, I need to keep going." I glance at the poster of my swifter hero, Cy Dennis, who's leading Iowa's team to the championship. "Besides," I add, "I'll need to be in good shape to compete."

"Jared Stringwood thinks your shape is fine." Sandra's got a smirk on her face. "You should see how he watches you when he thinks nobody's looking — even in virtual."

"Who cares what Jared thinks?" I try not to sound too interested, but Sandra knows me better than anyone.

"Tell it to a hole in the ground," she says, flipping her hair behind her ears. "Say it out loud, Leanna. Repeat after me: *I'm hot for Jared.* Come on, girl. It won't hurt. Say it."

Sandra's right about Jared. I do sorta like him, but I'll never admit it. At least not yet. "Go back to running," I say, dismissing her for being annoying.

"Did you hear this one?" Sandra starts to laugh, and I know a joke is coming. "What do clones do for fun?"

"I don't know, but you're going to tell me, right?"

Sandra's holding back a snort — "They go *bald*-room dancing! Ha!" She cracks up and can't stop herself.

I laugh, too, even though it isn't that funny. Mom doesn't like me to tell put-down jokes, not even about clones.

It's hard not to laugh at clones, though. They are just so dumb. And what's the big deal about making fun of a manufactured humanoid that's no smarter than a microwave?

Sandra bounces off the bed. "Hey, a group of us are meeting at the Metropolitan Museum of Art in New York," she says. "About seven. Wanna come with us?"

"Can't do a virtual date tonight, San. Got to work on my final paper. You know, the paper that's due at the end of our history unit, remember?"

Sandra's one of those kids who can somehow go fringing and still manage to keep her grades up.

"You know me, Anna." San is the only person who calls me that. "I love to go virtual-traveling. I'll have that paper done by dinnertime," Sandra says, then her hologram vanishes.

While guzzling down an eight-ouncer, I pop a new power cell into my commglasses so at least I can pretend to be riding in the open air. Mom worries that I spend too much time in virtual. "Leanna," she loves to preach, "it would be good once in a while for your mind to experience things in the reality mode."

My answer is always the same. "Mom, you wrote the textbook on how a kid's mind responds to actual *and* virtual, so you should know that the experiences are both okay."

Mom is a big-shot child psychologist who writes online articles and appears on T shows as an authority on children's mental health. She runs a clinic with her longtime friend Dr. Anatol Ayala, whom I've always called Doc Doc. Robert Chu, a dentist, and two nurses, Horace and Sheva, are also part of the clinic team. With Mom and Doc Doc they've built the clinic into the best one-stop-for-all children's medical facility in the Midwest. Just about every kid in the neighborhood goes there. And everybody loves Mom and Doc Doc.

All my grandparents are dead, so Doc Doc is the perfect stand-in grandpa. He's also the dad I never had.

I don't remember anything about my real father. I do know the facts about how he died.

When I was three years old, my whole family was in a farcar crash. My dad died in the crash along with my twin sister, Lindsay. Mom and I survived. Although I was banged up horribly, Doc Doc pulled me through.

I think about my dad a lot and try to remember anything I can about him. Mom tells me Dad was a big swifting fan. Somehow, working out and polishing my swifting game helps me feel closer to him.

For the last ten minutes of my workout, I start to kick it up, so I'll be totally ready for swifting tryouts. My endurance has improved over the summer, and my offensive moves are stronger. I somehow think my dad is helping me, even though he's not here.

The tryout is coming up in a few weeks. If I make the team, Mom has promised me a new pair of swifting gloves. So today I'm pumping hard. It feels like hot needles are piercing my legs. *Just five more minutes*, I tell myself.

That's when I hear the front door burst open, followed by Mom's scream.

"Leanna!"

I hear Mom give the house computer the codes to activate our security system. All locks are recalibrated instantly. Windows sealed. Shields snapped into place. Utilities switched to secondary. It's all happening so fast. I try to make sense of things.

Who's attacking us?

From the day we installed our house security system, Mom has insisted I learn the protocol. We drill once a month to make sure I know what to do if our house is ever breached. I've never really taken it seriously. It's more like fun, similar to the fire drills we had at my old school.

The metallic voice of the computer whirrs. *"The house is secure."*

I listen by the door. The click of Mom's heels on the tiles tells me she's running down the hallway. She stops at my bedroom. "Open up," she whispers.

"Not until you give the password." Those were *her* instructions. *Don't let anybody in, not even me, until I give you the password.*

Mom sighs. "You're right, Leanna. Okay, *with liberty and justice for all.*"

I snatch open the door. Mom rushes in and slams it behind her.

"What's going on?" I ask. "Is it a malfunction?"

"No, Leanna, it isn't." I can sense the agitation in Mom's voice, even though she's working hard to hide it. I want to be calm, too, but there's a ball of fear at the base of my spine, creeping up my back like a closing zipper-lock bag.

Holding my eyes in her gaze, Mom speaks to me carefully. "There is a terrible man coming from the Clone Humane Society. He's a bounty hunter named Joe Spiller, and he's ruthless!"

I shake my head. "The Clone Humane Society — why?" It's all so stupid but I giggle! There is no happiness in the sound. I'm just so scared. Talk about dumb! "Mom, you of all people wouldn't own a clone! This is crazy."

Mom doesn't answer. She's listening for Joe Spiller.

Suddenly, the house trembles, and a voice rushes forward. "This is Joe Spiller speaking, First Agent of the Clone Humane Society. Dr. Annette Deberry, for being a member of the treasonous organization known as The Liberty Bell and for conspiring with aliens to destabilize the global economy, you are under arrest. Surrender or be taken by force."

My mind is leaping from thought to thought.

Aliens? The Liberty Bell? Then it comes to me. This stuff is from a twenty-first-century graphic novel series in which time-sliding aliens called The O and members of The Liberty Bell Movement use clones and a cyborg army to hold Earth hostage and steal all the resources. It's a good series, but any preschooler knows it's all fiction. How come we haven't heard about these aliens before? Right?

The idea is so ridiculous, I laugh again, but there's nothing funny going on. The laugh feels heavy, like it's pushing something down. "Mom, this is so *let's pretend*. Tell Spiller The Liberty Bell Movement doesn't exist."

Mom won't look at me. "I can't, Leanna," she says quietly. "You weren't supposed to find out this way."

Something inside me flings open. That heavy thing that was a laugh pushes even harder; this time it makes me cry.

Mom wipes tears from her eyes and from mine.

"Graham's responsible for this," she says. "We knew it was coming, but not this soon."

I know right away — Mom is talking about Taylor Graham, who's just been elected High Chancellor of The World Federation of Nations (WFN).

I back away from Mom and lean against the wall.

Mom speaks to Spiller through the house computer. "The Liberty Bell stands for peace, justice, and freedom. When did such goals become subversive?"

Spiller's voice comes quickly. "Since you decided to take the law into your own hands."

I listen closely to Spiller.

He says, "If you want to identify with a bunch of Seconds, that's your right. But you cross the line when you take sides with aliens who are against your own kind."

Mom blurts, "By whose authority do you make this arrest?"

Spiller bangs on the door. "High Chancellor Taylor Graham," he says.

I am confused and furious. In my own frantic thinking, I try to piece it all together. It's a nightmare that makes no sense.

Earth has made voice contact with beings from other planets. A big space launch is planned for the following year, but no aliens have actually been on Earth. So who are The O? And why would my mother get involved with a radical group like The Liberty Bell Movement? Mom isn't a traitor.

I cry out like a little kid. *"Mom!"*

She hugs me. But even in Mom's arms, I can't stop trembling. We continue to weep and hold each other.

Between sobs, I ask, "Please tell me you aren't one of those extremists who want to build a clone-and-cyborg army to destroy the world."

"Absolutely not," Mom says. "What you're talking about is a comic book production. What I am is someone who doesn't believe in slavery or segregation."

I pull away. The knot in my stomach makes a turn. "Do you believe clones should be freed and cyborgs should be given equal rights?"

Mom nods.

"Then you *are* an extremist!"

"If that makes me an extremist, I'll wear the hat. But we like to think of ourselves as *abolitionists*."

"Like Harriet Tubman?" I say.

"People thought Harriet was an extremist, too." Mom tries to help me understand, but the lines aren't connecting for me.

"The early abolitionists fought to abolish slavery of *human beings*," I argue. "Clones are *not* human beings."

There is disappointment in Mom's eyes. I've never expressed my feelings about clones this strongly. I've never had to. My contact with clones has been limited to one — Deuces, Sandra's family domestic. This is the only clone I actually know.

"Clones are flesh and blood — same as you and me," Mom says.

"Those manufactured creatures are *not* human like us," I say.

The computer security announces: *"Two minutes, three seconds until the house will be breached."*

"I don't expect you to understand anything now," Mom says. "And I don't have time to explain." Her dark eyes are filled with uncertainty. "Hold your questions, Leanna. For now, all I need you to believe is that your father loved you and I love you."

The best I can do is nod and try to stop crying. Mom hugs me again, tighter this time.

"Trust me, Leanna," she says.

I promise that I will.

Spiller growls at Mom through the house computer. "If you're innocent, then submit to a mind probe and clear yourself."

"Never," Mom shoots back quickly, her hands shaking. "I will not submit to questioning on some trumped-up charges."

"I'll give you one last chance. Surrender and come along peacefully," Spiller demands.

Spiller doesn't know Mom the way I do. She's tough. She won't back down. Her courage has kicked in. This gives me hope.

Mom speaks firmly. "*Surrender* suggests I've done something wrong, and I haven't. I will never give up."

Spiller says, "Dr. Deberry, you leave me no choice. We are coming in." I slide down the bedroom wall and pull myself into a ball.

The computer's voice is back. "*My sensors reveal Spiller has two biobots. It will take the biobots one minute, thirty-one seconds to override the house security system.*"

Terror rises in me fast. *Spiller's got biobots!*

On the danger scale, biobots are ranked with rattlesnakes.

Mom's voice is soft but strained. "Leanna." She pulls me to my feet. "Put a few things in your backpack — hurry."

I do what Mom says, absently stuffing things I might need. I start with my commglasses, but Mom takes them from me. I quickly throw socks and a hairbrush into my backpack.

All the while, I'm trying to remember the T program I'd seen about biobots.

At first, they were created as simple toy pets, made from scrap metals. They ate garbage that they efficiently turned into fuel. Great concept, until bounty hunters like Joe Spiller customized biobots and programmed them to be killing machines that devour their victims, mostly stray animals and defective runaway clones.

A wave of nausea settles in my stomach when I let myself think about what biobots would do to Mom and me.

"This is your scrapbook," she says hurriedly, downloading files into my commglasses. "I'd planned to give this to you when you turn sixteen, but we don't have that luxury now. When you view the information, you'll understand, maybe not right away, how special you are. But most of all, I hope you know how much I love you."

Mom touches my cheek and kisses me on the forehead before tucking my commglasses safely into my backpack's inside pocket.

"Come now," she says, pulling me to the window that opens to the deck, which spans the back of our house. "There's not much time."

Mom needs me to act brave, so I try not to crumble. Tears keep coming.

Then I realize Mom isn't coming with me. I'm to go without her! I shake my head violently. "*No!* I won't leave."

The idea of biobots makes me squeeze Mom's hand tighter.

But Mom pulls away. "Your safety is the most important thing right now. If you're safe, that'll be enough for me."

Mom is willing to face a bounty hunter and flesh-eating monsters to make sure I'm free.

"Why is my safety more important than yours?" I argue. "We'll run together."

"Stop, Leanna!" Mom says. Then, holding my shoulders with firm and steady hands, she speaks to me, soft but steely. "How many times have we been through this drill? I need you — really need you — to step up right now."

"But I'm so scared."

Mom shushes me. "Daughter, I know I'm asking — begging — you to do something far beyond your years. I know you're frightened. I am, too. But I need you to do what I say without an argument."

Mom commands the computer to drop the protective shield from my bedroom window. "Go, now. Do just as we've practiced. Run!"

Just before crawling out of the window, I grab my dad's memory stick off the dresser and stuff it in my backpack. It's all I have left of him.

As I go, Mom whispers, "I love you, Leanna."

The computer announces, *"The house is disarmed."*

Mom has always told me that I am to go straight to Doc Doc's house if there's ever an emergency. But fear keeps me frozen. From where I am, I can hear everything. Those biobots growl so loudly. They ask, "You want I should give it a laser blast, boss man?"

"Not yet," grumbles Spiller. "They want Deberry alive so we can find out what The Liberty Bell is planning."

Following Spiller's command, the biobots rip with their teeth. Shards of furniture fly from the window.

Spiller's voice bellows Mom's rights. "Annette Deberry, cease to resist. You're being arrested. You have the right to remain silent. You have the right to an attorney . . ."

"This is nonsense," Mom says. "The Liberty Bell is trying to help you."

"We don't need your misguided help," says Spiller. "The arrest warrant says you have a daughter, Leanna Deberry. Where is she?"

"I don't know," Mom says softly. "I hope she is far away from this place."

I feel guilty for not obeying Mom — I should be at Doc Doc's now, but I can't bring myself to leave this spot.

One of the biobots asks, "Want we should look for the girl, boss man?"

Spiller is silent. "The warrant says nothing about the girl being under arrest, too."

I hold my breath and listen closely.

Spiller says to Mom, "Who would have ever thought you were a Bell Ringer?" Then, with a burst of anger in his voice, "What makes you stupid people think Seconds and Metal Heads are equal to human beings?"

Mom's tone is even, calm. "Clones *are* human beings. We have proof of this," Mom insists. "Graham knows we aren't conspiring with The O to take over the world. For almost four centuries, The Liberty Bell has been delivering The O's messages to humanity and working hard to keep liberty alive."

"You people think you always have the answers to what's wrong with the world." There's disgust in Spiller's voice. "And little green men have all the answers."

"As a society, we need to clean up our act or be prepared to pay the consequences," Mom says. "And killing the messenger won't change a thing."

Spiller grunts. "What kind of mother are you, putting pathetic clones and filthy, no-good cyborgs ahead of your daughter's safety?"

"I owe you no explanation for my actions," Mom says, still calm and even. "Arrest me and let's go."

Spiller chuckles wickedly. "After a penetrating mind probe,

you'll tell us *everything* we need to bust up this Liberty Bell group."

I blink to chase away the image of Mom getting a mind probe. If they drain Mom's brain, she'll be a vegetable.

More than anything, I want to jump back through the window and fight, but I'm not that kind of brave. I press myself harder against the trellis and stay out of sight.

I hear the biobots chewing, spitting, belching.

Spiller leads Mom away. I sneak to the side deck to get a view of the front.

Spiller's fartruck has brought neighbors out to see what's going on. Nothing this exciting has ever happened on Roseland Street. People gather on the sidewalk, milling around between Federation signs advertising the swearing in of Taylor Graham. Mom never supported Graham. Now I know why. One of Graham's campaign promises was to capture and prosecute dissident organizations. Seems The Liberty Bell was at the top of his list.

Our neighbor Mr. Briley yells from across the street. "What's going on? Annette is a good citizen!"

"We're not enthusiastic about bounty hunters around here!" yells Donna Baker, one of Mom's friends.

I quietly move behind the bushes by the side of the house, trying to stay hidden. They're putting Mom in Spiller's fartruck, and I panic.

Will I ever see Mom again? Will she be the same when they finish probing her mind?

There are still so many questions. The possible answers tear at my heart.

Still, I can't make myself go to Doc Doc's. Instead, I go next door to Sandra's house.

Mrs. Jaffe, Sandra's mother, pulls me inside the back door. "Get in here, girl," she says. "What's happening? You look like you've seen a ghost."

"They've arrested Mom." I start to cry.

"Who? For what?" Mrs. Jaffe goes to her front door, where she sees the crowd gathered on the street. She shakes her head, not fully believing what she sees.

Spiller scowls at the people gathered outside. "Go back to your houses. This ain't your concern. Don't make trouble for yourselves."

For the first time, I get a good look at Spiller. He's a large man with a stocky frame. His bald head makes it hard to tell where his neck begins. The tattoos on his face, arms, and hands are symbols popular with military troops. There's a vibo-gun strapped to his shoulder and an antique hunting knife in a holster on his hip.

The biobots bounce beside Spiller in a defensive pattern. I've never encountered what people call "tech-hounds" up close. They look like floating bowling balls with eyes on top of antennae. Mounted between the two spheres is an ebony screen that opens and closes. Behind it is the dreadful biobot mouth filled with razor-sharp teeth. There's an all-purpose util-ity belt filled with electronic tools and weapons around the middle of their round bodies. They operate with a number of retractable appendages.

I stand behind Mrs. Jaffe, looking at these disgusting things from over her shoulder. One of Spiller's tech-hounds snarls.

The ebony data screen rises, revealing jagged teeth and a long, slobbering tongue that scoops up a sparrow under a bush.

I stay quiet behind Mrs. Jaffe.

"Don't fret, Annette, I've got Leanna," Mrs. Jaffe shouts.

I can see the disappointment on Mom's face when she sees I haven't gone to Doc Doc's house. When Spiller's fartruck pulls away, taking my mother, something collapses inside me.

Mrs. Jaffe looks shaken. She is quiet, thinking. She gives me a smile although it looks more like a smirk. Mrs. Jaffe is not one of my favorite people. She is so check-the-box perfect. But today, I am grateful for help. "Leanna, come now," she says.

"Where's Sandra?" I ask.

"She's out on her bike." I'm eager to be with my friend. "When will Sandra be back?" I want to know.

"Soon," she says, glancing at the window. "Stay here with #222 while I see what I can find out."

I run to Deuces and drape my arms over the clone's shoulders. Her model number is 222, but Sandra and I always call her Deuces.

The clone pours me a glass of milk and smiles. "Drink."

I push the glass away.

"Happiness is milk. Gives teeth a pretty smile." Deuces is so cheerful. She seems unaware of the tension that is everywhere in this home. She goes back to peeling potatoes.

I wish life could be as simple as Deuces makes it sound — as simple as the milk in front of me.

I try to figure out what to do next. So many questions come at me, all at the same time, it seems. *Should I go to Doc Doc's or wait for Sandra to get home? Will Spiller and his biobots return to look for me? What is this Liberty Bell Movement?*

Doc Doc will have answers. I head for the back door and open it slowly, forgetting that Sandra's house, like many homes on this street, has a sensor for door security that makes a quiet tweet when doors are opened under everyday circumstances.

Mrs. Jaffe comes from the family room when she hears the door. "Leanna, where are you going?" She takes my arm. "You musn't leave now. It could be dangerous for you." She leads me back to the kitchen. My mind is too clouded to give her flack.

I go back to the milk Deuces has poured me and quietly decide to wait for a better time to run off to Doc Doc's.

I take a sip of milk. Deuces, who is still at it with the potatoes, hums happily. Dumb clone. She doesn't have a clue that something is not right.

Everyone I know looks down on clones. T programs depict them as on the same level as monkeys and well-trained dogs. My friends think they are the dumbest creatures that walk upright. The only person I've ever heard speak in defense of clones is Mom. Ever since I was a kid, Mom's been pro-clone. She once signed a petition to get an international law passed that would abolish clone ownership. Even though the bill was killed in the House Committee on Clone Affairs, Mom has always done what she could to improve the lives of clones.

Ugh! It is *so* embarrassing when Mom starts preaching power-to-the-clones in front of my friends! I must admit, sometimes I've wondered what's up with my own mother. Now I know.

I watch Deuces carefully. I'm all for equality, but really, what does Mom see in those pathetic losers?

As Deuces keeps humming her mindless song, I look for signs of humanity — anything that would show me clones should be free.

Nothing about the way Deuces looks convinces me. All clones in a series appear alike because they're made from the same cell donor. Even though it's considered an honor to have your cells generate a series of clones, I can't think of anything more creepy than hundreds of color-coded human-oids walking around with *your* features.

The Topas Corporation, manufacturer of clones, has no shortage of people who want to be donors. Topas even holds contests to choose new donors. The cells of movie star Jeanette Alexander were used to clone Deuces' 200 series. Each clone has something that is all its own. For Deuces, it's a smile that's as pretty as Jeanette Alexander's.

Other than that, clones are all the same. Without hair or eyebrows, Deuces, like all other clones, looks androgynous. They're usually called "it," even those that have strong male or petite female features.

No matter what anybody calls Deuces or any clone, there's no way a clone could ever be mistaken for human. Aside from being just plain dumb, other features that set clones apart from humans are their color codings and the numbers they're given according to model. Deuces is a domestic clone, so her skin and matching bodysuit are powder blue.

I've known Deuces since Sandra and I turned six, but sitting here watching her, I realize how little I know about what makes a clone tick.

"Deuces," I ask, taking a slow sip of milk. "Do you eat?" I'd never seen Deuces take in any food or even drink a glass of water.

"Yes," she answers. "Deuces eat what's left after."

Table scraps? Something feels wrong about that, but Deuces doesn't seem to mind. She smiles like Jeanette Alexander and winks. "Too much food makes you round in the tummy."

I then start to wonder about other basic needs. I've never seen Deuces sleep or heard anybody say she was sleeping. Whenever I'm in the Jaffes' house, no matter how early or late, Deuces is in the kitchen, cooking or doing housework. "Do you sleep?" I ask.

"Yes, there is a comfortable bed in the basement. It gets cold down there sometimes, but a plastic liner makes it warm." This sounds miserable, but Deuces talks like it's just the way it is.

A cold plastic bed in the basement is no biggie for Deuces. It seems so unfair when there are two warm empty bedrooms upstairs. I try to convince myself that Deuces is a clone and that clones don't have the same needs as humans. They can get by with less because they don't expect much. A sudden question comes to me then. "Deuces, do you daydream?"

Deuces looks puzzled. "Dreams come when sleep comes at night. No sleeping in the daytime, so no *daydreams*."

Without daydreams, Deuces has no imagination, unlike humans.

"Deuces," I blurt. "Would you like to be free?"

Deuces stops peeling potatoes. "Free to do what?"

"Free to come and go as you please. To do whatever you want. To live on your own."

Deuces sets down her peeling knife with a sudden firmness. "No — no such thing should get in a clone's head."

I can't stop pushing for an answer. "What if someone came along and said, 'Deuces, we're going to lead you to freedom.' Would you go?"

Deuces covers her face with both hands. "The Clone Humane Society decommissions corrupt clones. Please stop talking like that. It's too scary."

I've pushed too far. "Sorry, I didn't mean to upset you," I say.

"No more scary talk." Deuces speaks as if she's about to cry. "No more talk about free stuff."

"No more," I say. Deuces is like a pet or a machine. She needs to be kept small and out of the way. And, like the three million other clones made by Topas, there's no way she's ready to be free.

Just then, Sandra comes through the back door. She looks frightened. "Leanna, all the neighbors are talking. Thomas, from down the street, said you were here." My friend is talking fast. "Is it true? They arrested your mom?" She takes off her biking helmet and straddles a kitchen chair.

"Yeah, my mom belongs to a group called The Liberty Bell," I explain.

Sandra's eyes go wide. "Like the one in the old comic books about aliens called The O?"

"You got it."

Sandra shakes her head like she can't believe what she's hearing. "So are we now supposed to believe in time-sliding aliens who know our past, present, and future, all at one time? That would be frisk if it *was* true."

"Hey, you're the one who believed that the *Star Trek* T series was real history," I say, teasing Sandra.

"Ah, but don't forget. For years you thought the superhero Light Man lived in your lamp." Sandra laughs, and her giggle makes me laugh, too. I'm so glad to see her.

"Aw, c'mon, I was five years old!" I say.

"Seven!"

Then we're suddenly quiet.

Sandra sighs and cuts me a look. "Hey, Anna, it's me, San. What's up with your mom?"

"I don't know much about what's going on." I finish my milk. "The Federation has ranked The Liberty Bell as a treason-ous organization, and they arrested Mom. She says The Liberty Bell members are not extremists but more like abolitionists."

"*Terrorists*. That's heavy stuff with sauce on the side." Sandra shrugs. "*Abolitionists?*"

"Yeah, but that's the strange part. Clones aren't like American slaves," I say. "Slaves were human, at least."

"But remember what we've learned in Ms. Jamison's class. Back then, some people didn't think so."

I nod. "Yeah."

"Remember the articles we read by Thomas Jefferson, the ones saying Africans were inferior beings who didn't have the mental capacity to learn?"

"San, the slaveholders wanted to believe Africans weren't human to justify keeping them enslaved," I say. "But clones *aren't* human. They're manufactured."

Sandra cuts her eyes at Deuces. She lowers her voice. "Maybe clones have more to them than we think."

"So you're saying my mom and The Liberty Bell group is right and the whole world is wrong?"

Sandra shrugs, but she doesn't answer.

"Not likely," I say.

I fold my arms and lay my head down on the table. I have a headache. "All I know for sure is that Mom's in deep trouble."

The sound of Deuces' cooking fills the spaces of our talk.

Sandra rests her head on her arms, too, and we're facing each other.

She touches the scar on my left hand, a reminder of the farcar wreck that almost took my life. "I want you to know, when this story breaks about your mother being arrested, our friends are going to evaporate."

"I know." And I start to cry thinking about all of this. Sandra hands me a tissue.

"But we're girlenes, best friends for life. You're like a sister to me," Sandra says softly.

Mrs. Jaffe hurries into the kitchen just as Deuces is getting ready to process the potatoes. "Go do something upstairs," Mrs. Jaffe orders the clone. Deuces obeys and scurries away.

"I wonder sometimes if they aren't smarter than they act," Mrs. Jaffe whispers after Deuces is gone. "Leanna, I've made calls to several important people in the Clone Humane Society," she says. "Things are much worse than I thought. It seems your mother is being charged with belonging to a treasonous organization known as The Liberty Bell." Mrs. Jaffe sounds disgusted. "How could your mother be so mindless?"

Sandra steps in. "Mom, that's not fair. Leanna doesn't know anything about this Liberty Bell thing."

"Really?" Mrs. Jaffe sounds doubtful.

I bite my bottom lip. It's hard for me to lie, especially to Mrs. Jaffe. "No," I answer quietly.

Mrs. Jaffe softens. "Of course. Annette would never endanger her child by belonging to . . ." Her voice trails off. Now she's trying to make sense of it all, jumping back and forth between what seems impossible to believe and what seems possible to believe. "I knew Annette had radical thoughts, but I never would have suspected she was . . . was . . . a traitor."

"Mom," Sandra snaps. "Dr. Deberry is no traitor."

Mrs. Jaffe throws up her hands and shakes her head. "This will be settled in a court of law. Right now, the Child Protection Agency has been notified and they'll be here any minute to pick up Leanna."

I jump to my feet. I have to get out of there. "I should leave now."

Mrs. Jaffe takes my arm and tries to make me sit down. "Sorry, Leanna. You were ordered to stay with me until the authorities come. If I let you go, I'll be breaking the law."

"No!" I yank away hard and bolt out the back door, running blindly, stumbling, then falling hard before scrambling to my feet.

There's blood coming from my scraped knees. I will myself forward. *Get to Doc Doc's house!*

I hear Sandra behind me, hollering, *"Run, Anna! Go! Go! Go! Go!"*

I'm four blocks away before stopping to catch my breath. I ease into a slow trot. *Don't act suspiciously*, I tell myself.

I have not taken a sky tram, even though it would have gotten me to Doc Doc's faster. Too many people ride that thing, and I don't want to risk being caught by Spiller and his monsters.

By using side streets, I make it in half an hour. September in St. Louis can feel like a swamp. I'm exhausted and wet from sweating. I climb the front steps of Doc Doc's old mansion and lean hard on the doorbell. I'm tired and light-headed from the heat. Doc Doc looks so glad to see me. "Come in, Leanna." I half stumble into the foyer and collapse in Doc Doc's arms. He steadies me, and I let myself relax.

"I'm so glad you arrived in time." Doc Doc leads me into his study. "I got word that Spiller arrested Annette. That means that soon they'll come for me."

"Are you a part of The Liberty Bell, too?"

He answers without hesitating. "I am."

I haven't seen Doc Doc in several weeks. I'm shocked by how old he looks. He's a tall, slender man with hands and feet too large for his body, but as he shuffles along in front of me, his shoulders cave. His head is slightly off center and extends forward. The curly hair that frames his nut-brown face is an unruly salt-and-pepper mix. Doc Doc has always had a grandfatherly look, but now he seems elderly.

His frown is deep. He doesn't look at me when he speaks, which sounds as if he is expressing his thoughts rather than talking directly to me. "When they finish probing Annette's brain, they'll know how extraordinary you are and come back to find you."

Mom had said I was special, and now Doc Doc is saying I am extraordinary. They both know I do well in school and am a popular kid, but they've never used words like *special* and *extraordinary*.

I fall into an overstuffed chair in Doc Doc's office. "If being special brings on bounty hunters, later for that. I'm just fine with being plain old Leanna Deberry, an ordinary thirteen-year-old eighth grader."

Doc Doc chuckles. "You've never been plain or ordinary in your life." Then getting serious, he says, "You're probably feeling very confused, child." He reaches out. "Give me your commglasses. I want to download a scrapbook. Not all will be explained, but this will reveal many things."

"Doc Doc." I begin with the first of a million questions. "Why did you name your organization after comic book characters?"

Doc Doc starts slowly. "The Liberty Bell is over three hundred and eighty years old. For two centuries we were a secret organization, working anonymously. Then in the late twenty-first century, we were infiltrated. So instead of dissolving the group, we decided to hide in plain view. A publisher who was a Bell Ringer began producing a series of graphic novels that told our story from the days of Ben Franklin."

Doc Doc seems so relieved to be telling me this. He keeps on. "The public loved the graphic novels, but they didn't think any of it was true. They read the story as fiction. Then it became part of the oral tradition. All over the world, storytellers made the tale a part of their performances, but the plot and characters changed. The O grew more sinister and The Liberty Bell became criminal. It made for good drama, but very little of it was true. The popular movie won all kinds of awards, but the screenplay did more to damage our image. So did those violent virtual games."

"Don't forget the Halloween costumes, bed comforters, and all kinds of cyber junk," I add. "Some of that stuff is still around."

I remember a toy O ring Sandra once gave me for my birthday. Mom didn't approve of the O ring, but she let me keep it anyway. "The ring can help you slide up and down the ribbons of time," she'd told me. All make-believe, but I used to imagine what it would be like to travel to past events, visiting people and places. My love of history began with that silly little ring.

Doc Doc is eager to tell me more. "We were able to continue our work in secret because nobody believed The Liberty Bell existed. We're not doing anything that's harmful to our planet or the people on it. But still, folks believe we're evil."

Even if what Doc Doc said is true, I still wonder about The

O. The word is that they're a powerful force. But I've never been fully sure of who they are or what they want. There has never been any formal first contact made with any aliens, not even The O. Why now? Have The O shown up? All I know is what the mythology says about this mysterious force.

My head is killing me. There's so much to take in. I suddenly remember that I haven't had dinner, and I find my way to the kitchen to wolf down a peanut butter and jelly sandwich.

Back in his study, I watch Doc Doc busily transfer files from his computer.

I love the leathery smell of his office. Unlike the rest of Doc Doc's house, which is state-of-the-art modern, his study is a reproduction of a mid-twentieth-century library, complete with oversize leather chairs and richly carved wood furnishings.

I slide back into one of the big huggy chairs and let my eyes scan the room. As a little kid, I imagined that a dragon protected Doc Doc's books, and a book bear by the name of Professor Pages read to Doc Doc, the same way Mom read to me.

My favorite fantasy was about Teensy, the tiny book elf who made her home on the top shelf of Doc Doc's bookcase. These were my childhood fantasies.

Suddenly, a life-size bear dressed in academic robes materializes by the fireplace. "Hello, Leanna."

I am startled. It's Professor Pages! I don't have on my commglasses, so I'm not in virtual. When I touch him, he's solid, so he's not a hologram. Fantasy in the real world! Is this some new program Doc Doc's created? I look to Doc Doc, who gives me no clue, only a broad smile.

Professor Pages opens a large book. "Here are some people you might enjoy meeting," he says. Like a table of contents, there's a roster of names.

I recognize many of the people from lessons in school.

1. Gandhi, a twentieth-century nonviolent peace advocate
2. Morgan Templer, a late twenty-first-century peace negotiator
3. Cymbric, a prison reformer
4. Dr. Martin Luther King, Jr., a civil rights leader of the 1960s

And there's a line that says, "The Original Custodians."

"Who are Custodians?" I ask, going back to my comfortable chair.

"Those who were first contacted by The O and their descendants," Professor Pages answers. "They were the keepers of the words."

"What words?"

"Let them tell you."

Suddenly, an older woman dressed in mid-twentieth-century clothing enters the room and sits opposite Professor Pages. I don't need to be introduced.

I stand up sharply, and all I can think to do is something very corny. I curtsy! "Hello, Mrs. Roosevelt."

"Hello, my dear," Mrs. Eleanor Roosevelt says, telling me to be seated. Her face is as warm and friendly as the portrait of her that hangs over Doc Doc's fireplace.

"I read about you last year in school," I say, feeling proud of myself. "You were First Lady of the United States."

Professor Pages graciously introduces a man standing by a table near Mrs. Roosevelt. "May I present Justice John Marshall Harlan of the United States Supreme Court?"

Justice Harlan looks so distinguished in his black robe. Suddenly, Teensy the book elf flutters to my shoulder. "And sitting by the window," she whispers in my ear, "is your great-grandfather, Dr. David Montgomery."

I bound off the chair. "Freeze program!" I'm searching Doc Doc's expression for some kind of explanation. He's still smiling as broadly as ever. "Doc Doc, this is so . . ." I'm trying to find the best word.

"What is it you kids say?" Doc Doc asks. "*Frisk?*"

"Right! But this is better than frisk. What *is* this program?" I examine the figures that are now lifeless mannequins, like the ones I'd seen on a virtual tour of Madame Tussauds wax museum in London.

Doc Doc explains. "Teensy, Professor Pages, and all the rest are biographs."

"Like holograms?"

"No, holograms are different. Biographs are a lot like the ones you're accustomed to in virtual. A hologram is a three-dimensional picture that breaks up when it is touched and it can only exist in virtual. The biographs are the best of both technologies. Touchable, realistic replicas that can exist in the material world. Here, touch one," Doc Doc says.

"I don't need to wear my commglasses to engage them?" I ask, reaching out to touch Mrs. Roosevelt. She feels like a living, real person.

"No," he answered. "But if your glasses are on, then the biographs have been programmed to respond to voice command — your voice."

I am listening, and also studying the biographs. The tech is fascinating, especially the details of their faces.

"I've been preparing this program since you were born," Doc Doc tells me. "Your folks and I knew you'd be full of questions that we might not be here to answer, so we've downloaded centuries of information into these reproductions of key players in The Liberty Bell Movement. Ask them anything you would ask your mother or me."

"Can I start right now?"

"Sure. Talk to them."

Doc Doc leaves me. He goes back to working on his computer files.

I give the command. "Program, run."

"Mr. Benjamin Franklin, at your service," the biograph says, straightening his long colonial jacket and three-cornered hat. He pushes his glasses back up on his nose and continues. "Let us help you find the truth in the fiction that surrounds our story. I am the founder and first Custodian of The Liberty Bell. I started it in 1787."

Mrs. Roosevelt is next to speak. "For nearly four centuries, we Custodians have passed *our* story — not the fictionalized version of it — from one generation to another."

"This is exactly as it happened," Ben Franklin continues. "Philadelphia. July 1787. I was in the upstairs bedroom of a house on Market Street near the State House. We'd been working all day drafting the Constitution of the United States, and the South Carolina delegates had worried my brain over the issue of slavery. I was exhausted and longed for a good night's sleep. I was about to blow out the bedside candle, when two sinister figures rose up at the foot of my bed. I wiped my eyes and blinked. 'Hallucination. That is all!' I remember saying.

" 'Don't doubt your sanity,' the visitors said to me in a reassuring fashion.

"Mustering my courage, I thrust the candle into the darkened corner to see better, and called out, 'Friend or foe? Devil or angel? By what magic did you enter my locked chamber?'

"'We mean you no harm.' The two beings melted into the shadows."

At this point, Justice Harlan takes up the story from Ben Franklin.

"It was April 1896 when the visitors came to me. I was reading the briefs on the *Plessy v. Ferguson* case about segregation when The O appeared in my office. 'State the nature and intent of this intrusion!' I said, placing my pen in the silver inkwell on my desk. My hands were shaking from fear. 'Take what you will, thieves, but I — I have no money,' I said to them.

"The mysterious specters tried to reassure me. 'We mean you no harm,' they said."

Mrs. Eleanor Roosevelt continues the story from there.

"It was January 1943 and World War Two was raging. I was working at my desk in my bedroom when I felt a presence. 'You just can't walk into the White House private quarters,' I said, pausing when I realized that two intruders had done just that — walked into my bedroom straight through a solid wall.

"I pulled myself tall, as I'm prone to do in stressful situations, and spoke with more confidence than I felt. 'You must know there are guards right outside my door. All I have to do is scream.'

"'We mean you no harm,' said the strangers."

Next, Dr. David Montgomery begins his part of the tale.

"I was working on my doctorate degree at Northwestern University in August 2088. Two mysterious intruders appeared in the lab where I was studying late. 'Did the Topas Corporation send you?' I asked. I rushed to put myself between them and the prototype of my adult-cloning machine. I shouted, 'I'm not selling my invention. Go tell them that!'"

Now the story is Franklin's again. "I asked who they were and where they had come from. 'Our kind are everywhere,' they said as one. 'Your word observers seems to best fit who we are. We watch and observe and try to keep order in our sector of the Universe. We have a name, but you would not be able to pronounce it. Please just call us The O.'"

I jump in. "What did they say they wanted?" I ask, anxious to find out.

Mrs. Roosevelt shushes me. "Hold on to your questions until you've heard the whole story, otherwise you might miss something important."

As hard as it is, I promise to be a good listener as Mrs. Roosevelt continues.

"The O said, 'We come with a warning and a message. The message is this: In 2171, humankind will have mastered the technology necessary for intergalactic space travel. Unfortunately, from what we see in the future, you are not ready. But heed our warning: Unless all life-forms are free on your planet, we will have no choice but to stop you. You must become a Custodian of your world.'"

Ben Franklin interjects. "To me, it was witchcraft! But The O explained, 'There is no sorcery involved. We are appearing to you in 1787, to Justice John Marshall Harlan in 1896, to First Lady Eleanor Roosevelt in 1943, to Dr. David Montgomery in 2088, and to a nameless girl in 2170, all at the same time.'"

I ask Ben Franklin how such a thing is possible.

He explains. "The O said, 'There are countless pasts, presents, and futures, all recorded on grids, like ribbons that stretch into infinity, so the future is fluid. As decisions are made and problems solved along the grids, future outcomes are ever changing.'"

Dr. Montgomery jumps in with a slap of his thigh.

"Spherical time! One of my professors studied the whirlpool theory for years. He would have died a happy man if he'd known about The O."

While I listen, I remember the O ring Sandra gave me for my birthday when I was a kid. In my memory of that little toy, I can still imagine the ribbons of time in my mind, moving pictures of our history overlapping, fast, slow, but always moving.

I keep very quiet. This whole experience is impossible to believe unless it happens to you. I'm so glad this part at least is happening to me! The story returns to Ben Franklin.

"I asked The O why they'd chosen me to visit. They answered by saying, 'Liberty, freedom, and justice are not easy for young civilizations to achieve. So we have stepped into Earth's history when ideas such as freedom and justice are attainable goals. We hope you will start a new ribbon that will lead to a different future than we see — a better one.'"

Benjamin Franklin looks over the tops of his glasses. "And that is why I started The Liberty Bell," he says.

Mrs. Roosevelt says, "There's one more thing that concludes our story. Before The O left, they also gave us a message, but we've never understood it. Still, we have passed it to every Custodian since."

"What did they say?" I ask.

Benjamin Franklin, Mrs. Roosevelt, and Dr. Montgomery answer at the same time: "They are not rocks."

My head is about to crash from overload. I ask, "Why didn't The O make first contact with High Chancellor Graham of The World Federation of Nations? Or our President Livingstone?"

Mrs. Roosevelt says, "We believe it's because Graham is not open to new ideas of liberty. Graham has chosen to be our enemy, and The O know this. Livingstone is Graham's ally, so he is equally ineffective in moving forward the cause for freedom."

"Who is the nameless girl The O told you about?" I ask.

"We don't know," says Justice Harlan.

Doc Doc ends the biograph program.

"Totally frisk," I tell him.

"And there's more to all of this," he says. "We are in 2170, and our work is not yet finished. Graham is planning an inter-galactic launch next year, and he is arresting all Liberty Bell members so that nothing stands in his way. Everything now depends upon the last Custodian — the girl who has no name. None of us knows who she is."

Doc Doc takes my hand. "Enough for now, Leanna."

They are not rocks? The mysterious words echo in my thoughts.

Doc Doc sits down next to me. He chooses what he says carefully, like he's offering me an important lesson.

"The program is saved in your commglasses. The people you've just met — Benjamin Franklin, Mrs. Roosevelt, Justice Harlan, Dr. Montgomery — are your travel companions. They can help you, guide you."

I nod, feeling the power of this.

Doc Doc explains. "Down through the years, The Liberty Bell Movement has taken unpopular positions to keep justice alive. Our antislavery beliefs were met with great resistance in the 1800s. Just as the liberation of clones and cyborgs is one of our unpopular issues today, we've fought to get rid of segregation, colonialism, and terrorism, along with human suffering all over the world."

Doc Doc beckons me with his hand. I follow him to the large kitchen, where he opens the pantry door and presses a remote control. A false wall swings open, revealing hidden steps that lead to a lower level and a circular staircase that spirals down to a floor below that.

"Come," Doc Doc says. "We must hurry. You go first."

Doc .Doc hands me a glow stick and coaxes me to keep moving forward. The hidden wall, stairs, and narrow passageway seem familiar somehow — like my escape from slavery earlier today.

Now I am running again, into the unknown.

Using our glow sticks to light the way, we proceed before coming to a metal fire door. I'm eager and terrified.

Doc Doc finds a key on top of the frame and unlocks the entry. This way of doing things is so twentieth century, but I trust Doc Doc and stay close to him. There is another hallway up ahead. We follow it to stairs that take us to a trapdoor that opens to an abandoned carriage house one street over from Doc Doc's property. "Hurry," he whispers.

We make our way to the upstairs apartment over the garage. The quarters are small but neat and well equipped.

"Who stays here?" I ask.

"Whoever is in need," Doc Doc answers.

A yawn comes quickly. I am *so* tired.

"Rest, Leanna," Doc Doc says. "Lie down here on the couch and count backward, slowly, from one hundred to one."

With this monster of a day over, I need no help falling asleep, but I count anyway for Doc Doc's sake. He's loved this counting game ever since I was a little girl. I can see it makes him happy that I am willing to play.

I'm asleep before I get to seventy-five.

When I wake up, I silently pray that it's all been a nightmare.

Mom's preparing breakfast. Soon she'll be on me about taking too long to get dressed.

I rub my eyes and feel Doc Doc's couch beneath me.

This is no dream.

Doc Doc sits at a table across from the couch. He's talking casually to a clone. I've never seen a First and a Second chatting comfortably like friends. *Strange.*

I sit up and stretch.

"You slept all night. Good," says Doc Doc. "This is #9767. He's your porter to safety."

Right away, I notice the clone's skin is orange, which means general laborer. And Doc Doc is calling the clone "he," same as the Jaffes, who call Deuces "she." There are some things I won't do. Clones are "its"!

With downcast eyes, #9767 waits for me to acknowledge it.

"Good morning," I say, trying to smile. "Glad to meet you."

"Thank you, Miss Ma'am."

Doc Doc says, "Leanna, it's time for you to go. #9767 is

going to take you to a place unknown to anyone. The less I know, the less Spiller can coerce from me with drugs and mind probes."

The room feels suddenly cold. I hug one of the couch pillows to my chest.

Doc Doc says, "This clone was sent anonymously to help us. I don't even know who his First is, which is good. If I knew, it might somehow lead to your future hiding place, and this information can be pulled from me."

"Aren't you coming?" I ask Doc Doc, fear rising in my stomach.

"No, I'm going to wait for Spiller. Your mother and I have been in this together all along. She shouldn't have to endure this by herself."

I glance at #9767.

"Everything is in place," Doc Doc tells the clone. "Taylor Graham is making good on his campaign promise. He's coming after us with all the power of his office."

"Who we got on our side?" asks the clone. I wonder how this orange being can think so well for itself.

"That remains to be seen," says Doc Doc. "Liberty Bell members are everywhere. When our case reaches the US Supreme Court, there's no telling how many Bell Ringers will reveal themselves. But right now, it is best for members to stay hidden."

"Yes." The clone nods. "Ready to go?" it asks.

"No," I say with pleading eyes. How could Doc Doc ask me to go off with a strange clone to an unknown place?

"I know this is difficult, Leanna. We didn't plan it this way, but we need you to cooperate," Doc Doc says.

He's not convincing. In his firm but loving way he whispers, "So much depends upon your safety. Now go. Use your bio-graphs when you have questions or need advice."

"When will all of this be over?" I ask. And then, like a little kid, I say, "I want to see Mom."

Doc Doc doesn't answer. He waves good-bye as #9767 and I step out into the quiet morning.

In the distance, I hear sirens wailing and coming fast.

When we get to the Midwest Gypsy City, I am hungry. I soon lose my appetite.

Gypsy City is a smelly, ugly place, a 350-foot hover barge that is a floating junkyard. People come to buy salvage — broken electronics, recyclable fuel cells, robots, and rebuilt robots. Some of the stuff is legal; most of it's not.

City dwellers looking for a bargain flock to these hover barges by using sky trams and farcars.

This morning, the Midwest Gypsy City is hovering beside the Gateway Arch, 630 feet in the air. The Midwest waits for authorization from a Missouri Department of Commerce, River Traffic Division agent before it can move downstream to Natchez, Mississippi.

We ride in on the sky tram and dock on Level 4. Signs point to the cargo bays on levels below us and levels above. The clone rushes us to Level 5, where a long line of shoppers are crazy-mad when they see #9767 getting off the elevator.

"Where have you been?" one customer complains.

"We've been waiting all morning," says another.

"This is not the way to run a business!" a third person shouts.

"Are you beginning to corrupt?" snaps another.

The clone patiently listens to the complaints, never saying a word back to anyone. Putting on a utility belt, #9767 pulls me aside. "Be still," it whispers. "Don't call attention to yourself."

Now I'm as annoyed as these other people. I yank myself away. "Did you just give me an order?" I snap. "Has your program been corrupted, or what? Clones don't *give* orders; they *take* them!"

#9767 is quick to answer. "No, ma'am. Not giving orders. Just being careful, that's all."

"Okay," I answer, taking a seat on a nearby bench.

The clone opens the doors for business, and customers pour in from the parking level.

I manage not to scream when three fierce cyborg land trekkers zoom in on their bikes.

I've seen trekker bike races on the T, but I never thought I'd get to see real trekkers up close.

The leader of the trekker trio steps back, eyes me, and growls. I refuse to show how scared I am. I look at him straight and hiss.

"Well, little sister," he says with a laugh, "you've got claws." He flashes me the trekker sign for solidarity and walks though the checkout door with his items, complaining the whole time.

"The price for recyclable fuel cells is too high. We need less dependency on tech-energy," he shouts.

His fellow trekkers applaud, and he keeps it up. "Twentieth-century basics like fossil fuel are where it's at."

"You're a Neanderthal," another customer shouts. "Fossil fuel almost killed our planet."

The trekker scoffs, then leaves with his buddies.

As the people in the crowd shove one another to get to merchandise, a voice rises above the din. "Hold on a minute."

A commerce inspector pushes to the front. "Cease all business," he screeches. "This junk pile has to be inspected."

The crowd opens up to let the inspector pass. My clone greets him without ever looking into his eyes.

The inspector introduces himself. "I'm Mason Beckley."

"#9767, sir, property of Captain Jack Newton, master of this vessel."

Beckley's wearing an expression like something smells bad. "I'll be honest with you," he says. "I'm not accustomed to doing business with a Second. But your First's permissions seem to be in order. Captain Newton trusts you to run this dump when he's absent. His lunacy, not mine."

Beckley's a little man who makes himself smaller by flaunting his authority. He's determined to find something wrong. He opens and shuts containers and sliding doors. He rifles through bins, looks under furniture, and searches for anything in violation of a commerce code. An entire inspection usually takes days. I worry that we'll never launch, but Beckley focuses his attention on only the open sections. He eyes me and #9767 as he goes. *Will he inspect us next?*

"There's something about this whole floating junkyard's operation that bothers me," he says. Beckley's eyes stare hard, back and forth between me and #9767.

"I don't like the way Captain Newton lets you run the place," he says to the clone. "Where is Newton anyway?" he asks.

With its body bent and head bowed, #9767 answers. "Captain Newton is on urgent business in Minneapolis. He'll join the craft by the time it arrives in Memphis. He left orders."

Beckley says, "You better not be lying, clone. Are you covering up for Captain Newton?"

I speak without thinking. "Clones don't have the ability to lie."

#9767's eyes cut to me quickly, and I know my mistake. I've called attention to myself by talking back.

Beckley gives me a superhard look. "And who are you?"

"My name is . . ."

#9767 does something clones aren't supposed to — it jumps in to speak ahead of me, a First. "This is Captain Newton's niece, sir. She'll be going all the way down to Natchez."

A lie, I think. Even though clones don't lie, this one does. *Has this clone been altered? Is it corrupting?*

Beckley's eyes have not left me. "Niece, huh? What did you say your name was?" I shift on my feet.

"Her name is Beatrice Newton, ID# 770-65-5030," the clone answers.

"Shut up, Second," Beckley says. "Let the girl speak for herself."

"So sorry, sir. Just doing what the captain says to do. Taking care of everything his niece needs."

Now Beckley's hawkish look is on #9767. "There's something not quite right about you."

"Sorry, sir." #9767 lowers its eyes.

I don't like Beckley, but I secretly agree with him. There is something different about this clone.

Clones aren't capable of being deceptive, but this one is. Someone has illegally altered #9767's systems. I feel sure of this.

Beckley looks from #9767 to me, then back again. "At first glance," he says, "I'd suspect Gypsy City would be in violation of at least twenty codes. But surprisingly, your cargo and credentials are in impeccable order. You are an efficient manager, a credit to your First."

Beckley keys his approval into the barge's central computer. The main engines come to life, allowing Gypsy City to continue its journey.

Beckley says, "You know what the word is about these Gypsy City barges. Some folks think you're part of an illegal underground. You wouldn't know anything about that, would you?"

Silence.

Beckley puts on a pair of commglasses. "You ain't as dumb as you look, Second." There's a smirk in his voice. "I'll be watching you, #9767."

Beckley pushes past me, then he backs up. "Why aren't you in school, Beatrice?"

A lie slides off my tongue so fast. "My mom is sick. She's sending me to live with my grandparents in Natchez."

Beckley gives a command to his commglasses. "Show Beatrice Newton."

My eyes shoot to #9767, which won't look at me.

Beckley studies the photo ID of Beatrice Newton, then looks at me carefully. "Yes, I see that your grandparents do live in Natchez, on Tyme Street. You are one of their five grand-children. Natchez is a good town. You'll like it there." He manages an approving smile, then leaves.

I breathe slowly. *Relief.*

As soon as Beckley and the crowd are gone, I ask #9767, "How did my picture show up as Beatrice Newton?"

The clone doesn't answer. It starts to walk away from me. "I asked you not to call attention to yourself!" the clone snaps.

I run to catch up with it.

"Hey, you just referred to yourself as *I*. And did you say you asked me not to . . ."

". . . call attention to yourself."

"That's not how a Second talks to a First! Something's not right here!"

I follow #9767 down two flights to Level 3, then down a hall-way, past the kitchen, and into the staff's quarters. The clone opens a compartment and pulls me inside. "It isn't first class, but it's safe," the clone says, adding, "Need anything, call the cap'n down way."

It closes the door and leaves me there alone.

My heart sinks fast. I am surrounded by four dingy walls. A cot, table, and straight-backed chair look even uglier under the white light overhead. This is worse than a twentieth-century prison cell.

My peach-colored bedroom seems a million miles away. So does talking with Sandra about Jared Stringwood. So do Mom and Doc Doc. And everything that brings me comfort.

I sit on the sagging cot. Even in this awful place, it feels good to be quiet.

I'm wiped out. I stretch out on the cot and slide into a nightmare.

A biobot is about to bite off my head. I am running, hollering, calling Mom's name. Spiller has turned into an orange clone and is riding on my back, telling me not to call attention to myself. And there's Beckley, hooking me up to a lie detector, while #9767 looks on and laughs wildly. Doc Doc is the captain of Gypsy City. He's the inspector, too, looking at everything around us.

Harriet Tubman flies out of nowhere, chased by a whole army of biobots.

I wake up screaming, hugging myself to stop the shaking.

Then, like a gentle hand helping me somehow, I remember my memory stick, way down in my backpack, under my clothes. It is the last thing I'd packed but is now the first thing I need.

I touch the tip of the cylinder to activate its images. One by one they appear on the gray walls around me: Daddy's smiling face, his eyes in thought. Unlike visiting with Daddy in a virtual setting where I interact with him, the memory stick allows his memories to speak to me without words, just feelings.

The images flood my being, and I feel the emotional power of Daddy's thoughts soothing me. I experience the same joy my father felt when he held me in his arms for the first time. I love hearing Daddy's heartbeat as he watches me take my first step as a toddler. His pride is my pride. His loving concern comes into me when he watches me sleeping or tucked in the covers when I have a bad cold.

"Daddy . . . Daddy . . ." I smile and let Daddy's precious memories wash over me. Even though I've used the memory stick many times, the results are especially good today. "Thank you," I whisper before deactivating the stick.

Wearing Daddy's love like an invisible coat, I'm ready to look at my scrapbook, which Mom has downloaded.

With shaky fingers, I adjust my commglasses and give a voice command. "Virtual mode, Leanna's scrapbook."

Entering a virtual program from a lying position makes me nauseous. Even though the chair is criminally uncomfortable, I use it to anchor myself.

"Play program."

Mom's face appears in virtual. *She looks so real.* I gasp when I see her and run to greet her. "Oh, Mom," I cry, "it's been terrible."

My urgency makes me pass through the image and disrupt the transmission. Mom has used an outdated V-2 scrapbook format, probably done when I was a little girl. So many improvements have been made since the V-2 was introduced. Now Mom's image is laced with static.

"Welcome. Come in," the V-Mom says. "It is time for you to know the truth."

I try to look past the poor reproduction. I'm happy to be close to my mother's image.

"Leanna," she says softly. "I had planned to share all of this with you in person when you were older and better prepared. If you are here, then it means, unfortunately, that our plans have been altered. I am so sorry, but you need to know who you are."

There is a swirl, two clicks, and the scrapbook opens. In my virtual mother's loving voice, the one she uses when she's soothing me after a letdown or bad experience, she narrates the pictures and bits of memorabilia.

"Leanna, you are my beautiful daughter, and I love you. I would freely give my life to protect and save yours. So would a lot of other people."

I want V-Mom to get to the part about The Liberty Bell and how I fit into it. But there's no way to speed up a V-2 scrapbook. It has to follow its programming. So I listen impatiently while Mom retells my whole life story. "You are named after my grandmother Sarah Leanna Montgomery. My grandfather was Dr. David Montgomery. I called him Pap-Pap."

"I know all that stuff already," I say anxiously.

The program sputters and clicks.

"Patience, child. You need to hear the whole story."

She continues my scrapbook. "When infant cloning was made illegal, your great-grandfather developed an adult-cloning replicator. The Topas Corporation bought the invention and used it to mass-produce a race of slaves. But the clones lived only twelve years because of their rapid cell deterioration. Topas made billions of dollars doing this. Meanwhile, Pap-Pap worked on a formula that would stabilize cell growth. This would have allowed infant cloning to take place safely again."

This was new information for me. "You mean Dr. Montgomery found a way for clones to last past twelve years?" I ask. "Why didn't I know about this?"

The program clicks again. Mom's image becomes jerky. "The Topas Corporation tested the stabilizer and said it was a failure. Pap-Pap knew better, but the corporation was too powerful for him to fight. So Pap-Pap hid his formula and waited. Topas Corporation didn't have to make clones look the way they do. Topas used gene manipulation and micro-chip insertions to control clone behavior and functionality. They seem more like androids than humans."

V-Mom has my full attention now. I pray the program will stop acting up, but the sputters continue.

"Pap-Pap's stabilizer had to be retested. We needed to make a baby that would grow and learn, same as any human child. No gene manipulation and chip insertions."

"But infant cloning is illegal, right?"

The program clicks several times over. I pound my fist on my knees.

"Be patient, Leanna," V-Mom says. "Let the story unfold."

"Where does *my* story begin?"

Pause. Click. Click. This lame program!

"I met Forest Deberry, your father, when he became part of The Liberty Bell Movement, but he was also the love of my life and the reason for my happiness. I'd never met anybody so thoughtful and kind, yet strong and disciplined."

I see the love in Mom's eyes, even with the bad imaging. Although she had stopped crying at night like she used to, I would sometimes see her using *her* memory stick.

"We did everything together," V-Mom continues. "We sat up many nights talking until we ran out of things to say, and then we stared into each other's eyes and talked without words. We were married six months later on a hot August day."

I never get tired of hearing how Mom and Daddy fell in love and got married. Then comes the *me* part. The V-Mom's tale is a parade of words, creating images that move easily, one after the other.

I know all of this is leading to something, and I'm eager. But there's an uneasiness creeping up in me, like the flash of lightning before a thunderstorm.

"Forest was the one who came up with the idea that The

Liberty Bell Movement needed to test Pap-Pap's stabilizer by cloning a baby. We knew such a project would be dangerous and illegal. And then there was the moral question of what would happen if the making failed and the clone child lived to be only twelve.

"During this debate, I discovered I was pregnant. Your dad and I decided to have twins — one a natural child and one a clone."

It took a moment for V-Mom's words to form a whole thought in my mind. "Wait," I say, facing the figure of my mother.

My heart is a hammer in my chest. "I know how Lindsay and Daddy were killed in a farcar accident. But you never told me Lindsay was a clone."

Suddenly, the program features a colorful biography of Lindsay's short life with me. The two of us are running through the yard. Riding ponies. Swinging. Swimming. Pillow fighting in our matching pajamas. We were identical in every way.

"Mom, why did you keep this secret from me?" I ask. "Why didn't you trust me? It's okay if Lindsay was my clone."

Pause. Click. Click.

"No, Leanna. It's the other way around. Honey, *you're* the clone."

Suddenly it felt like all the air had been sucked out of the room.

A punch in the stomach. That is what this news is. A fist to my gut.

The other way around! Leanna . . . you're the clone.

My tears seem to be laced with acid — oh, do they sting.

"Are you saying . . . I'm . . ." I force myself to spit out the words. ". . . *a Second*?"

V-Mom nods. "Yes, Leanna, a clone."

I rip off my commglasses and hurl them against the wall. "It's not true!" I scream. "Stop saying that!" I pound the wall. "I'm *not* a clone!" I gag on my words. My throat feels thick, and I throw up.

"Clones are not human! *I'm human!*"

Staying in the same room with this news is unbearable. I have to get out of here.

Blinded by my tears, I run through the halls of Gypsy City like a wild mouse. I'm scared of what's behind me but even more terrified of what's ahead.

"Are you out of your mind?" a crew member says as I rush through the narrow hallway.

I push my way past Gypsy customers, down one corridor, then another, until I come to a gathering area.

"Slow down!" a shopper yells.

All eyes seem to be on me; it's like everyone knows what I've just learned.

This feels like a bad joke from a T reality show. An hour ago I was a regular kid. Now I'm a manufactured freak.

I keep running, wishing I could escape my own skin.

In the main lobby of Gypsy City, the T is blasting: *"Hear what the recently elected High Chancellor has to say about the arrest of two unlikely terrorists, Dr. Anatol Ayala, world-renowned pediatrician, and Dr. Annette Deberry, award-winning child psychologist and the granddaughter of Dr. David Montgomery. Both have been charged with treason because of their membership in an underground dissident group known* as *The Liberty Bell. Yes, folks, The Liberty Bell we thought was just a story turns out to be true! See it here first in the High Chancellor's own words. Program your T and commglasses for the six o'clock news here at TNCB with Anita Johnson-Armbruster as your host."*

I hate Graham, The Liberty Bell, The O, Mom, Daddy, Doc Doc, and everybody else who has helped create this mess I'm in.

After ducking into an exercise room lined with mirrors, I force myself to look at my reflection.

I look like any First with dark brown hair, brown eyes, and a halfway decent smile. *Nobody will ever know I'm a Second. I can pass.*

I have so many questions.

What if I start changing color?

Will my hair fall out?

Can I ever get married and have my own kids?

Turning to run again, my foot slips, and I slam headfirst into one of the mirrors. People rush to see what's happened. I assure them I'm fine, and they move on.

The mirror is made of safety glass, so I'm not badly cut. But the mirror is cracked, and my head is pounding.

There's moisture on my face, blood from a small cut over my eye. My blood is red. The idea makes me wonder. I inhale and let the air out slowly. I slide to the floor and lean against the wall.

Mom once told me that clones are flesh and blood like me, like a human. I shut my eyes tight and let my mind grab on to this tiny ray of hope.

A man's voice speaks to me then. "Hey, there, I'm Captain Jack Newton. You must be Leanna Deberry." He helps me to a chair.

"How many fingers do you see?" the captain asks.

"Two."

"Any blurred vision?"

I shake my head.

"Very good. I don't think you have a concussion." He examines the small cut. "We'll do a quick scan just to be sure you're not hurt badly," he says, handing me a pair of med-scanners.

They're worn like commglasses; I put them on. The captain has a pair, too, and slides them on over his eyes.

"Sir, is clone blood red like a human's?" I ask while the captain busily sets up the test.

"As red as a Martian sky. Be still now." The captain gives the voice command. "Scan."

The med-scanner activates and instantly sends a picture of my head to the captain's glasses, where the data is analyzed and a diagnosis is given.

"Was a nasty bump you took on your head," he says, studying the results. "But you'll be fine."

"I slipped," I explain, standing up to leave. But I'm too dizzy, and I sit back down.

The captain looks around to make sure we're alone. "I went by your room before finding you here," he says, handing me my commglasses. "I found these on the floor. The program was still running."

I take the commglasses, my eyes lowered. New virtual systems would have automatically shut off once I removed my commglasses. But Mom's outdated V-2 scrapbook doesn't. "Did you look at the program?" I ask.

The captain nods.

"Then you know about me?"

"Don't worry, I'm a Bell Ringer, too. But what if some enemy had found your scrapbook? The Movement could have been compromised."

"I don't care about The Movement right now!" I fix my eyes on the floor pattern. "Don't you people know it's illegal to make a clone?" I whisper through clenched teeth. "If Mom and Doc Doc are found guilty, they could be sent to the Mars penal colony!" The captain lets me talk. "My whole life has been a lie. The Liberty Bell could bring about freedom and justice because the all-knowing O told them to? I want no part of your Movement."

Captain Newton chuckles. "Leanna, you're just as feisty as you've been reported to be," he says. "You are a credit to your kind, and you're proof of our best argument — that clones are sentient beings."

"I'm not a manufactured doll or toy. I'm as human as any First."

"That's our point. You aren't like those concocted creatures Topas produces."

"But why wait until I'm thirteen to tell me I'm a clone? Wouldn't it have been better for me to grow up knowing? I should have been included in this scheme."

The captain says simply, "Security."

The answers are coming too fast and too easy, which makes me think everything's been rehearsed long before any of this happened.

The captain explains more. "A few of the top leaders in The Movement have known about you since the beginning, but for security reasons, we never knew your identity, where you lived, or whether you were male or female. That you exist is the only information we had.

"Your mother and Dr. Ayala played their roles well, pretending they were in the dark, too. They've kept you a well-guarded secret."

"They didn't even tell *me* about it," I say.

"Your mother made a wise decision, Leanna. Think about it. If you had known you were a clone, it would have caused *you* to place limitations on yourself, based on society's definition of what a clone is. You believed you were a First and acted like one, achieved as one. And you might have told somebody about your status. That would have been dangerous."

"I wouldn't have spoken to anyone about this."

"Are you sure there isn't one girl buddy you'd have shared your secret with?"

"No one," I say, thinking of Sandra and proving to myself that clones do lie. "I'm thirteen," I say, looking at my hands. "I'm still here. So Dr. Montgomery's stabilizer must be working."

My mind rushes back to my last physical.

"Everything looks great," Doc Doc had said.

He and Mom seemed way too happy about it. Now I know why. Their experiment was working. *Experiment. Lab rat!* Is that all I'd meant to them?

The mirrors positioned around the exercise room play tricks with my eyes.

While looking at myself, I morph into a bald-headed, orange clone. My long, thick hair is suddenly gone. When I blink, the image changes back to the human me.

"Am I going to turn a color or lose my hair?" I ask the captain.

"Absolutely not," he says with confidence. "Color coding and the androgynous look are features artificially programmed into the adult-cloning process by the Topas Corporation. There is no reason why clones can't look like any other humans. Topas doesn't want that to happen, though. If clones are proven to be human, then the Thirteenth Amendment to the Constitution, which abolished slavery in the United States, would apply to them also. That's where you come in, Leanna. You are the proof."

Just then, I notice the orange cuticles around the captain's thumbnails.

The next morning, Captain Newton takes me to breakfast. While I'm eating, I notice a sign over the counter: FOR GOOD HEALTH — SECRETS STAY SECRETS ON GYPSY CITY.

After a while, the captain introduces me to Houston Ye, a Gypsy pilot who shuttles merchandise between Gypsy cities on the Missouri, Ohio, and Allegheny rivers. "Meet Leanna Deberry," he says, nudging me forward.

Houston is nicely packaged. A cute guy with an athletic body. He smiles a lot and seems very friendly at first.

"This shuttling is just a temporary job," Houston explains as the captain settles us at a table in the private staff lounge. "Someday I hope to be a student at the Parks School of Aeronautical Science in St. Louis," he says.

I don't know much about aeronautics, but everybody knows the Parks School has a mile-long waiting list.

The captain turns to go. Before he leaves, he takes me aside. "Houston isn't part of The Movement, so watch what you say."

When the captain is out of sight, Houston's disposition changes. His smile dissolves.

"Got brothers and sisters?" I ask, trying to be friendly.

"Nope." Houston folds his arms and slides down in the chair.

I change the subject. "I go to a virtual school. We've been studying slavery and the Civil War. I was a V-runaway on the Underground Railroad with Harriet Tubman."

The conversation stays one-sided; Houston is as closed as a locked trunk. *Oh, no,* I think to myself. *He must know I'm a clone.* But I push that idea away and try to find something he wants to talk about. "What kind of stuff do you like doing?"

"Flying," he mumbles.

"Did you say flying?"

"Space pilot."

It's not easy getting Houston to talk, but he loosens up some. He tells me, "After I go to flight school and earn my galactic license, I want to start a transport business." When he talks about flying a spaceship, his smile comes back. "I'd love to go into outer space," he says.

Outer space isn't my favorite subject, especially since finding out about The O. But at least it gets Houston talking. I ask, "If you like space exploration, why don't you apply for admission into the Federation Space Program?"

"I'd never get in." Houston shuts down again. His smile is gone.

I'm about to excuse myself when I spot swifting gloves in Houston's open backpack. "Hey, are you a swifter?"

"Yeah, I'm a bubble chaser." His face brightens a little.

"Wish they had a swifting court here on board."

"They do," Houston says, all teeth and gums.

For a moment my life doesn't seem so heavy. "Want to take me on?" I ask.

"You betcha," Houston says. "Let's go — let's get animated!"

I hurry back to my room, grab my swifting stuff, and rush to where Houston has suited up and is waiting. We take the elevator to the lower level and make our way down a long hall to the last door.

"I play by Olympic rules," I say.

Houston straps on his gloves. "Federation rules."

"Don't know Federation rules, but I'd like to learn them," I say. "I'm going to try out for our swifting team at school next year." Then I remember — since my escape, there isn't going to *be* a next year.

Houston reads the disappointment on my face. "Hey, what's wrong? You're not having second thoughts about the match, are you?"

"No, no, not at all," I say softly.

I need to play this game. My troubles are still out there, spinning like a whirlpool ready to pull me under at any moment. But right now, I am getting ready to have fun swifting. I can pretend things are normal, just for this moment.

Swifting is a game I'm good at. "Get ready to get dowsed," I tease Houston. "And we can even play by your rules."

Houston laughs. "Pretty sure of yourself, aren't you?"

"Swifting is frisk," I say with certainty.

In the center of the floor is an official-size swifting chamber — fifty feet long by twenty-five feet wide by fifteen feet high. Houston switches on the lights. "Sorry, this is a manual court, not automatic," he says.

He explains the Federation rules of play. "The purpose is the same: to capture the water bubble in the back court and try to score a point by throwing it through one of the four goals on the front court wall."

"Got it," I say, checking my gloves. "What about scoring?"

We enter the chamber, which has become zero gravity, allowing us to float upward. We become suspended in midair and turn slowly.

Houston gives the scorekeeping details. "A player must retrieve the bubble and score within forty-five seconds, in numeric order. Five points, followed by the two ten-point goals, then the fifteen-point goal, and finally the thirty-pointer. Whoever reaches seventy points first wins the game."

"Simple," I say, practicing a difficult move to show off my skills. "What if I throw the bubble through the higher-numbered goal before the lower or drop it through a goal I've already scored?"

"You lose a turn," Houston says, snapping his helmet strap. "No hand blocking, just hip checking and head and leg blocking. No kicking or elbowing, either."

"Fair enough."

I win the coin toss, so I get the first catch. We touch gloves and take our starting positions. Cy Dennis, my favorite swifter, can control her movements on the weightless court better than any player I know. I've practiced some of her moves all summer, so I'm anxious to use them. My instincts tell me Houston is going to be a strong opponent who will test my skills. I like that.

It's always exciting floating at center court, waiting for the water bubble to be released. Water oozes out of the tube and immediately takes the shape of a bubble. It drifts over my head. Pushing off the side wall, I propel toward it but misjudge my force and crash into the bubble rather than capture it in my swifting gloves.

"Foul!" Houston shouts. "Two more of those and you lose your turn."

"I know! Okay!" I'm embarrassed. What a lousy start. I usually play better.

Water plunges from the tube and forms a new bubble. This time, I let the bubble float to me. Reaching out, I capture it with my swifting gloves. I turn toward the goal. Houston waits in the front court, ready to block any attempt I make to score.

My strategy is to do a flying triple flip, then dive for the first goal for five points. As I begin the move, Houston slides in and uses his hip to nudge me. In zero gravity, I go cascading in a downward spiral and almost open my hands. I could have lost the bubble, and Houston could have captured it and scored!

I push off the floor and shoot straight to the ceiling. The shot clock says I have ten seconds to score. Pushing off the side of the back wall, I stiffen my body into an arrow.

As I pass Houston, I use my shoulder to nudge him in the same direction I'm moving. This catches him by surprise, giving me just enough time to drop the bubble in the five-point hole.

"One of Cy Dennis's special moves," says Houston, nodding his approval. "Nicely done."

"You know about Cy?"

"Sure, I know about Cy. She's Iowa's best. Think they'll take the championship this year?"

"I'm pulling for them."

I'm feeling pretty frisk about my score until Houston captures the bubble in the back court, moves with total control into the front court, and scores before I have a chance to throw one hip check. I've never seen anybody with that much control on the bounce.

"Not bad," I say, trying not to act flustered.

We play round after round. What Houston achieves with body control, I achieve through acrobatics. Weightlessness is an equalizer. A thirteen-year-old girl can compete on equal footing with a sixteen-year-old guy because it isn't about strength or size. None of that matters in a zero-gravity swifting match.

Soon the score is tied forty to forty. Match point is coming up. I'd missed scoring during the last set, so Houston is up again, shooting for the thirty-point winner. The bubble releases. He captures it and immediately heads for the scoring wall.

He tries to pass me, but I use my foot to hook his legs and send him toward the back court, away from the goal wall. Pulling himself into a ball, Houston kicks out toward the goals.

To change his direction, I hip check Houston, who spins out of control. This slows him up just long enough for the shot clock to tick down.

Buzzz.

Too late. He's missed his chance to score.

My turn. Capturing the bubble, I move up to the top of the swifting court, hovering high above the goals. I wait for Houston to advance against me, but he protects the scoring wall.

The clock is ticking! I have to move fast. I kick off the ceiling, flip three times, and land on Houston's shoulders. Leaping off, I move forward while pushing Houston down and out of play. Although he tries to recover, it's too late. I drop the water bubble into the thirty-point goal.

"I win!"

Houston wipes his face with a towel. "Yeah, yeah, yeah! That was some maneuvering," he mumbles.

"Thanks!" And that is as good as I can expect from him.

After being weightless for forty-five minutes, we need to come back to normal gravity slowly, to avoid muscle cramps and dizziness. This swifting court is manual, so Houston and I strap ourselves into foldout chairs while we gradually return to normal gravity.

"Where did you learn to swift like that?" I ask. "In school?"

"They don't have swifting at my school," he says. "I learned from my brother, who slipped me in to play at his school."

"Why'd he have to slip you in?"

Houston looks at me straight. "You don't know, do you," he says. "I thought you were being nice because the captain told you to."

I blink. "What are you talking about?"

"Don't you know I'm a cyborg?"

"No way," I whisper.

It's so quiet and still in the swifting chamber that I swear I hear Houston's heart beating. I wonder if his heart is real or artificial.

I look at our reflections in the window across from the chamber. We have no physical markers that identify me as a clone and Houston as a cyborg. We look like two normal kids, friends, maybe, who've just finished playing a swifting game.

No two people could have been less likely to be friends, though. Humans and cyborgs don't mix. They live in separate neighborhoods and go to separate schools. Since the Moon was colonized, many cyborgs went there to live and to work in the mines.

The longer we sit there, listening to the quiet, the more I realize Houston doesn't fit into any of the horrible cyborg stereotypes I'd seen on the T. In fact, he wasn't so scary.

Cyborgs get as much bad stuff said about them as clones do. People think they're roughnecks — crude, rude, ugly, and scary.

"It doesn't matter to me if you're a cyborg," I say. "I'm not prejudiced." But this isn't true.

I'm just glad I don't have a truth chip inserted in my head like the clones that are made at Topas. The truth is, nobody likes cyborgs.

Houston gives me a hard stare.

I trace lines in the mat with the toe of my shoe.

"Most people *are* prejudiced against cyborgs," Houston says. "You know the saying — *you wouldn't want to be locked in a room with a cyborg.*"

This is like another bad T show, a sitcom this time.

I'm a clone passing as a First, claiming not to be prejudiced against a cyborg.

This whole thing makes me shake my head in disbelief. Houston misreads the motion. "Look, I don't need pity!" he says.

"I don't pity you."

Houston looks at me with a strange kind of understanding. "You seem different," he says softly. "Especially since you agreed to a swifting match. I should have known, nobody volunteers to play with a cyborg. They think we'll kill them, or worse, turn them into one of us."

"That's not true."

"Oh, that's right. We cyborgs lie all the time. Can't be trusted, right?"

"I didn't mean —" I stop, remembering my conversation with the captain. If I'd grown up knowing I was a clone, I wouldn't have tried to achieve. I swallow hard. "You're right. Houston, I probably *wouldn't* have played a swifting match with you if I'd known you were a cyborg. I would have expected you to beat me." I ask, "Was that a real game, or did you let me win?"

"No way," he answers quickly. "My strength and size have nothing to do with skill in a swifting match. You won fair and honest."

We're silent for a moment.

"Is your blood red?" I ask without thinking.

Houston frowns. "Where'd that dumb question come from? Of course my blood is red!"

Everything I say sounds ridiculous. "I've never met a cyborg before. . . ."

Shut up, Leanna, I tell myself.

Houston looks away. "Try to stop talking until we can get out of this chamber."

We are very quiet after that.

Finally, our bodies adjust to normal gravity. The timer buzzes and we are able to unstrap and exit the swifting chamber. The silence continues as we remove our gear and wipe off the excess water that clings to us from the game.

Houston heads toward the door. Pausing, he calls over his shoulder, "I was a *normal* boy once. Just like you — the all-American kid." His back is turned and I can't see his expression, but I can feel his distress. "Then the accident," he says softly, as if the memory is still agonizing. "Got banged up pretty awful in a boating accident. My two cousins died. They were the lucky ones."

Houston's shoulders sag. Then he continues, still not facing me. "We were in a remote area. A storm was coming, and there was no way out. I was dying. But because of my injuries from the accident, Mom wouldn't let me go. She insisted that Dad okay the necessary surgery to save my life. I have an arti-ficial heart, a bionic arm and leg, and a biofe eye, but yes, my blood is still red! But I'm three-fifths of a human being, so that makes me a cyborg, a Metal Head. Choose one of the many names they call us." Houston sighs and lowers his voice. "So much for normal."

"I'm sorry," I whisper.

I am surprised when Houston turns suddenly and shouts, "Sorry?! You have no idea what it's like to be called names and told you can't come into places because you're different."

"You don't *look* different," I say.

"But I *am* different." Houston rolls up his sleeve. On his forearm is a tattoo of a C within a circle. All cyborgs have them. "How would you know what I'm talking about? You're a privileged First."

Now Houston is acting like a stereotypical cyborg. "Don't be obnoxious!" I say, taking a chance that underneath all that anger, Houston is a nice guy.

Houston's eyes flash anger, then he pulls back. "I'm out of here." He pops on his commglasses and heads out the door. Within seconds, though, he is back. "Hey," he says, looking at me strangely. "You need to hear this."

Houston hands me his earphones. My hands tremble from the cold and the anxiety I am feeling. The news loop is on. A reporter breathlessly announces, "*Dr. Annette Deberry and her partner, the eminent pediatrician Dr. Anatol Ayala, were scheduled to be arraigned in US Federal Court on charges of sedition and treason on Friday morning. Right now, the authorities are looking for Deberry's daughter, Leanna Deberry, a thirteen-year-old who hasn't been seen since her mother was taken into custody. Anyone knowing the whereabouts of this young lady should call the local police right away. A reward has been posted in the amount of one million dollars. . . ."*

There is no mention that I am a clone — actually, that is the least of my worries. No doubt the authorities learned all about me when they drugged Mom and Doc Doc. A million-dollar bounty on my head means every bounty hunter with biobots will be tracking me. And just when I think it can't get any worse, it does.

"What makes you so important that the authorities would pay a mil for you?" Houston asks, eyeing me curiously.

I don't answer. The captain had warned me that Houston is not a part of The Liberty Bell. But I reason he is a cyborg and they hate the authorities. I need all the help I can get.

Houston slings his backpack over his shoulder and heads for the door again. "For that amount of money, I'd bet my last tooth and dollar that somebody on this junk heap has turned you in already. See you 'round, Million Dollar Baby."

"Wait, Houston," I call. "What should I do? Would you help me?" There is no turning back now.

Houston shakes his head. "Spoken like a true First!" he says. "I'm a cyborg. Life is hard enough for me as it is. I get called names. We're sent to separate schools. People constantly complain that we have an unfair advantage because of our strength, so I'm locked out of all sports competition. We're called Frankenstein's Children — undisciplined, disrespectful, unpatriotic, and just plain crazy. I have a biofe eye, so people are also afraid that I can see what's under their clothes."

"What's under mine?"

"Yellow."

My face gets warm. Houston doesn't seem to notice. He rushes on. "My biofe eye is off most of the time. My bionic arm and leg allow me to run faster and lift heavier things than most people twice my size. And my heart can slow down to twenty beats per minute . . . and still I live. Nobody wants a cyborg around until there's some dangerous job to get done, like Moon mining or ocean harvesting. My point is, why would I help you? Why would you even ask?"

I spit out the words. "Because I am a clone." Then I blurt out the whole story. "My parents cloned me from my sister, as an infant, so I grew up thinking I was a human twin, a First. I'm some kind of experiment that'll prove that clones have been robbed of their humanity. I am proof that a clone can grow up just like a First, and the Topas Corporation doesn't want that to happen."

Houston is stone still. He looks at me curiously.

"Okay, Houston, I know all this sounds crazy, but it's true," I say. "A bounty hunter with biobots is probably looking for me right now. I'm no match for them, but you would be. Will you help me?"

One look at Houston's expression and I know he's not going for it. "Why would you invent such a wild story? Is this some kind of test?"

"You gotta believe me!"

"I don't gotta do anything!" This time, Houston never looks back. "Nope! No way. I don't believe you're a clone."

"Why else would the authorities put a million-dollar reward on my head?"

Houston opens the door to leave. "Who knows? And besides, I don't really care. All of this is too strange for me." He flicks his hand like he is tossing away my words. "If you're really a clone, you're going to need more than my help."

Then he is gone.

I figure Houston is right. Somebody on Gypsy City has probably turned me in. I go straight to the captain's office. He tells me to sit in the hallway while he finishes doing business with a used farcar dealer.

The dealer stares at me like he's trying to remember if he knows me or not. He reminds me of a river rat, but I keep my head down and hurry away. At last, the dealer leaves. The captain calls me into his office and offers me a seat.

"I'm all over the web and T," I blurt out. "There's a million-dollar reward for my capture." I walk around to the side of the captain's desk. I feel so trapped in this junk pile. "Isn't there someplace else you could take me?"

"Hold on, calm down," Captain Newton says. "What's got you spooked?"

I am too embarrassed to tell him that I told Houston I am a clone. Mom and Doc Doc kept me a secret for thirteen years, and in less than a day, I'd told a total stranger — a cyborg — about my illegal status.

"Is there anyplace else to go other than here? It's just a matter of time before somebody is going to recognize me."

"Listen," the captain says patiently. He holds me by the shoulders. "Try not to let fear cloud your thinking. You're safer here than anywhere else. #9767 and I have it under control. Trust me."

The captain continues to work at his desk. He motions for me to sit down, which I reluctantly do.

"We've tried to think ahead of our opponents," the captain says. "They know now who they're looking for . . . but let me think."

"Am I moving to my next station?" I ask.

The captain shakes his head. "I can't say, Leanna."

"I know, I know," I say impatiently. "The less information we have, the less we're able to reveal if we get caught."

"Smart girl," Captain Newton says. "And they say clones can't learn. Like dirty dishwater, that idea needs to be thrown out."

"What's dishwater?" I ask.

The captain chuckles. "Look it up," he says, turning back to his desk.

While the captain is busy, I look up the term *dirty dishwater: murky water in which dishes have been washed by hand.*

It sounded like fun, *washing dishes.* I'd have to program a virtual to get the feel of it. It was hard to imagine cleaning dishes with water instead of sound.

The captain dozes off. Meanwhile, I play a game of V-tennis with Sandra. When I finish whacking her, I take off my comm-glasses and applaud my victory. There is no way I could beat the real Sandra in a live tennis match. But in virtual, all things are possible.

Suddenly, the captain wakes in mid-sentence. "Resting my eyes. Just thinking a bit," he says. "I've made up my mind, though . . . really I have . . . Just to be on the safe side . . ."

He is struggling. "What's so hard for you to say, Captain?" I ask, patting him on the back. "Just say it!"

"I'm going to hide you in my secret quarters."

The captain switches on the T screen and scrolls the remote to 29. On command, the wall behind his desk slides open, revealing a hidden room and a tiny bathroom, about fifteen feet square. Unlike my quarters downstairs, this place is laid out designer-style with antique furnishings, a well-stocked refrigerator, a T with a security screen, and a shelf of real books.

Captain Newton shows me how to use the remote to lock myself inside. "Most handheld scanners and biofe eyes can't see through the wall, and if discovered, it would take a person with a vibo-gun at least ten minutes to blast through the titanium walls. By then, you'd be long gone."

In the ceiling of the tiny bathroom there is a trapdoor. "It looks like a vent, but it's an escape route," the captain explains. "If you are discovered, use it to get away." Then he shows me how the security system works. "You can see and hear what's going on all over the craft, from in here or in my office."

I study the security screen and see the cafeteria, then the lounge, then the checkout counter, the cargo bay, everywhere.

"Looks like you thought of everything," I say.

The captain doesn't speak.

"Why didn't #9767 bring me here first instead of taking me to that dingy little hole downstairs?"

"These are *my* quarters, not #9767's," says the captain with a wink.

Then the captain gets right down to business. "We're going to hover for a few days. Can't move too fast or I'll raise the attention of the inspectors."

"Where is #9767 anyway?" I ask. "I haven't seen him lately."

The captain raises an eyebrow and smiles. "I notice you're referring to clones as he and she instead of it."

I don't know when it happened, but in my mind, I now accept the fact that I am a clone. I'm not a thing. I'm not an *it*.

I begin to settle into hiding. Although I can't leave my room, I don't feel like a prisoner. The little place is inviting because the captain has stocked it with so many interesting things. Portraits of the original Custodians — Ben Franklin, Mrs. Roosevelt, Justice Harlan, and Dr. Montgomery — hang on the wall. I wonder about the final Custodian and who she might be. Does that person know about me? Will we ever meet? There are so many pieces missing in The Liberty Bell puzzle. Trying to understand the work of a nearly 400-year-old organization isn't easy. Sometimes I feel like I am trying to build a house from the top down.

I look around my new quarters. I'm very surprised by the banned books that are on the antique bookshelf: *To Kill a Mockingbird* by Harper Lee, *The Hobbit* by J. R. R. Tolkien, and *1984* by George Orwell. My fingers trace the letters on the spine of *Frankenstein* by Mary Shelley and *Strange Case of Dr. Jekyll and Mr. Hyde* by Robert Louis Stevenson. I know about these books, but I have never been allowed to read them.

A cameo of Abraham Lincoln, the Great Emancipator,

hangs on a wall, reminding me of how hard it is to change things. It would take more than a movement to bring about the changes the world needs to satisfy The O. We need to have somebody in power, like President Lincoln, who has the authority to make it happen. It couldn't be Graham.

From the private room, I see the captain working at his office desk. "Can I please call my friend Sandra Jaffe?" I ask. "She would want to know I'm okay. She'll be worried."

The captain explains that commglasses are too easy to trace.

"Isn't there a way?" I plead.

"We'll see," says the captain. He closes the wall, locks me in, and heads for the door. "Stay here."

Not long afterward, I hear a soft tapping at the office door. I can see #9767 from the security screen inside my hideout. I open the wall.

"Here's a snack. Hope you're hungry."

I take a bite out of a sandwich. "You're in charge while Captain Newton is away?" I ask.

"Clones are never in charge. They are faithful servants," says #9767, watching me.

Silence.

"Do you know I'm a clone?" I ask softly.

"Yes." Even without hair and eyebrows, he's the image of the captain, only orange and bald. "You're the product of infant cloning," he says. "How lucky you are to have had a childhood. At least you were allowed to grow and learn without alterations to your genes. We adult clones are born without pasts, without memories."

"I would be lost without my memories," I say, thinking how lucky I am to have my father's memory stick.

"Exactly," replies #9767. "The captain knew somebody who worked at the Topas Corporation. He had me cloned from his own cells but put some of his memories into my making."

That explains why #9767 is different.

The food is good, even though it's simulated. I eat more as we talk. "I'm surprised the captain even owns a clone," I say. "The Liberty Bell calls clone ownership modern-day slavery."

"The captain needs me," he says. "I'm his eyes, ears, and legs."

//MyStory/Leanna/Personal
Real Date: Friday, September 21, 2170
Real Time: 5:55:02 pm
Virtual Date: Friday, July 3, 1863
Virtual Time: 4:01:20 pm and counting
Subject: V-Gettysburg, PA

I don't want to sound whiny, but I sure miss Sandra. "The captain won't let me call my best friend."

#9767 doesn't answer. He gives me a pair of commglasses. "Captain's orders were to give these to you. They're unregistered and untraceable — and illegal."

"I'm illegal!" We both laugh. I grab the commglasses and give the command. "Find Sandra Jaffe, AVS Missouri."

As the commglasses gear up, I hear the deafening boom of cannon fire.

The computer finds Sandra in a virtual program of the Civil War Battle of Gettysburg.

I cover my ears. I can't see what's in front of me. Smoke darkens the sky. My eyes burn.

I see Sandra running ahead. I call out to her. "Hey, girl. It's me."

"Anna," Sandra shouts. My nickname has never sounded better. "Where *are* you?"

"I'm behind you by the low brick wall." I leap to safety just as a Union soldier scrambles over the loosely stacked stones. He is close enough for me to see how young he is — not much older than the boys in my class — but clearly he is terrified. He uses his sleeve to wipe the dirt and blood caked on his face. There is grim determination in that young soldier's eyes.

"I've been worried about you!" Sandra says, jumping over the wall. She is crying. We hug tightly.

"I'm okay. I'm okay," I say, and start to cry, too.

The cannons fire again. Now both Sandra and I cover our ears to muffle the sound. More soldiers in blue scramble past.

The smoke clears long enough for us to see an officer in gray put his hat on and raise a sword high in the air. I remember reading about this battle. "That's Brigadier General Lewis Addison Armistead," I shout. "He's rallying his Confederate troops to charge. Let's just stay here by the wall. It'll be over soon."

We sit with our backs pressed against the cool stones while the battle rages around us. "Where *are* you?" Sandra asks over the screams and yells of the fighting men.

"I can't tell you because there's a million-dollar reward on my head!"

"I know. Joe Spiller came to our house, asking a lot of questions. He told me to call him as soon as I heard from you. He really thinks I'm dumb enough to do it."

It feels so good to be with my best friend, even in virtual. Suddenly, a soldier falls wounded in front of us. He is in such horrible agony.

"All of these young men are dying to end slavery," Sandra says. "You've got to ask why."

I try to make sense of it for Sandra. "It's like the class we had about the first WFN chancellor, Thomas Adu, who once said, 'People will fight to defend what they believe is right no matter how wrong it may be.'"

Sandra looks sad, like she's lost something familiar. "You sound so grown-up now. What is it?"

"I have so much to tell you."

"Why do the authorities want you so badly?"

I'm ready to blurt out my whole story when I remember that #9767 is there listening. "You'll find out in time" is all I say.

After leaving Sandra, sadness moves into my spirit like fog. I start crying, harder this time.

Before leaving the office, #9767 closes the titanium wall to the secret room and locks it with a jolt.

I need help, so I call for a Custodian. "Mrs. Roosevelt."

The First Lady appears, seated in the captain's recliner. "Oh, my goodness," she says after seeing my sad face. She pats my arm. "You've been crying."

"Do you know that I'm a clone?"

"Dr. Ayala has made sure that we know very little about you. We knew you had a secret that would weigh heavily on your soul. But no, we weren't aware that you are a clone."

"And it doesn't matter to you?"

Mrs. Roosevelt says tenderly, "Why would it? I'm a biograph. Dr. Ayala programmed me to support you, not to pass judgment."

"I've got a million-dollar bounty on my head. Somebody's going to turn me in, and I'm so scared. I miss my mom and Doc Doc. I've never felt so alone." I take deep breaths to keep more tears from coming.

Mrs. Roosevelt hugs me. "When I was at Allenswood Academy in England, I sometimes felt lonely. But I had friends and teachers who cared deeply for me. Leanna, I want you to understand that you are surrounded by people who love you."

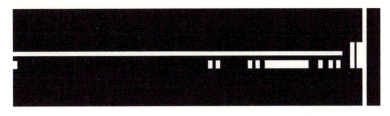

#9767 wakes me up with breakfast, the way he has the past few mornings. He busies himself doing things in the office.

I turn on the T. *"Seventeen more people have been arrested and more warrants have been issued for members of the infamous Liberty Bell Movement, including Howard Grange, of the US House of Representatives,"* says the T reporter, breathless with excitement. *"As questioning continues, more arrests are expected."*

"Look," says #9767, pointing to the news ribbon running at the bottom of the T screen. There is a message to me. *Leanna Deberry. Please call internet ID #10.1110.11562 to speak to your mother and Dr. Ayala.*

"Is this a trap?" I am fighting hard to stop fear from taking over my thoughts. "What should I do?"

#9767 is quick to answer. "Use the untraceable commglasses."

"Are you sure?" I don't fully trust that a clone can make such a decision. "What if they know how to trace the untraceable?"

#9767 opens a file behind the captain's desk. He pulls out the pair of commglasses. "Illegal," he says. "They can't be traced."

I put on the untraceables. Although this will be only an audio transmission, #9767 adjusts the sound to make sure there's no background noise that might give a clue about where I am.

"Remember," whispers #9767, "your mother and Dr. Ayala are in custody and might not be able to control what they say. Give them nothing."

I issue the verbal command. The commglasses connect me to audio. "Mom, are you there?"

A beep comes quickly. *"Voice recognition verified; now transferring to Deberry."*

"Hello, Leanna," Mom says. The tension in her voice is thick, but I let her words wrap around me like a quilt. "I miss you so, so much!"

It's strange talking without a visual. I so want to see my mother, but hearing her will have to do. Mom is reserved, but I can tell she is happy to hear from me, too.

I let Mom carry the conversation.

"Leanna, have you looked at your scrapbook?" Mom's question sounds so far away. "Finding out about being a clone that way had to be devastating. I promise it will be better once you turn yourself in."

Mom is struggling to speak. *Is she talking through clenched teeth?*

"Turn myself in?" I swallow hard. My mind can't make sense of it. Is this really Mom? "I've talked to Ben Franklin and Eleanor Roosevelt and the others," I say. "They wouldn't want me to give up."

Suddenly, a man's voice comes through. "Leanna, this is Dr. Ayala. We're glad you're keeping up with your lessons, but you'll do as you're told. Tell us where you are and we will come for you."

Doc Doc would never call himself Dr. Ayala to me. And he doesn't seem to understand the importance of my conversations with Ben Franklin or Eleanor Roosevelt. He thinks they're school assignments. "Do as I say, do you understand?" he blurts.

Doc Doc wouldn't throw out impatient demands like this.

"I hear you, Dr. Ayala," I answer. I would not call him Dr. Ayala in a normal conversation. This is all so strange.

Mom's voice is back. "Dear, turn yourself in, and we can put all this ugliness behind us."

Dear? Mom never uses words like *dear* and *darling*. She is signaling me, letting me know she is not speaking for herself.

"Do you think I'm stupid enough to swallow that pig?" I shout. "My mother and Dr. Ayala would never ask me to turn myself in."

Just before I disconnect, I hear Mom let go with a loud victory whoop.

I silently pray that these commglasses are truly untraceable.

The wall between my hideout and the captain's office is open. #9767 busily rubs the neckline of the captain's shirts with Insta-Kleen Power Cleaner. It's strange that he is wearing gloves. Clones don't need to. He is in a talkative mood. He tells me Houston is back after making deliveries to the Ohio River Gypsy City.

"Why are you telling me? I don't care." But I do care, because Houston knows my secret.

A knock comes on the captain's door. From the door's small top window, I can see it's Houston. I'm almost happy to see him . . . just to say thank you, but #9767 insists that I go to the hidden room and close the wall. "Just in case," he says. For safety, I agree to go, but I want to stay and see Houston.

Once inside, I use the security screen to see everything going on in the outer office.

Houston pushes his way inside. "Where's Leanna?" He sounds eager, too.

Now #9767 is dusting. "Somewhere. I don't know," he says sharply.

"Nobody has seen her for days. I've been asking," says Houston. "Tell me, what do you know?"

"She's not here. You know clones can't lie."

Suddenly, a man who looks like a character in a very dark movie frames the door. He's not a big guy, but his presence fills the office. He's fully bearded, with a shock of white hair that hangs to his shoulders. A bulbous nose punctuates the man's face. He inspects the room. Walking from item to item, he touches everything. It's as if his fingers can somehow gather information. His prominent forehead serves as an awning for his small black eyes, which move constantly, always searching. It's like he's hunting for something smaller and weaker to pounce on. Scary.

Though his tailored suit might tag him as a businessman, his hands are a giveaway. They're gnarled and twisted, and several fingers are missing on each hand. Even more frightening is the C within a circle tattooed on the back of one of his hands. A cyborg. It doesn't take much to figure out this man is probably a bounty hunter, and Houston has brought him to Gypsy City to capture me. I should have known Houston couldn't be trusted.

Houston scans the walls with his biofe eye. "I don't detect anything, but I can't get a good read. There's too much titanium," he says.

For the moment, the titanium keeps me safe. I stand still. The slightest noise might lead them to my hiding place here behind a wall, a few feet away.

"Come here, Second!" The man grabs #9767 by the collar of his bodysuit. "Do you know who I am?" he asks.

"No, sir."

"Listen to my name carefully. Li Rizin. It will be the last name you hear unless you tell me where Leanna's hiding."

"I don't know, Li Rizin. Sir."

"Did you use the first-person pronoun, *I*?" Li Rizin hisses. "What clone speaks of itself as an *I*?" He lifts #9767 with cyborg strength. "I've been hearing weird stories about clones that don't look or act like clones!" He slams #9767 against the wall with a thud. "What is your number?"

"9767," the clone answers.

Li Rizin looks suspiciously at #9767.

The clone says, "You know we are programmed not to lie, don't you?"

"Yeah, but . . ."

Rizin hurls #9767 across the room. The clone falls into the bleach he'd been using to clean the collars of the captain's shirts. Some of it splashes on #9767's arm, and suddenly, the orange coloring fades. The clone tries to hide it, but it is too late.

Houston grabs a tissue and dips it in the cleaner. My heart is beating so, so fast. Houston and Rizin rub off some of the orange skin on #9767's arm, and that's when I see — it's Captain Jack Newton! I use all the strength I can hold on to, to stay hidden.

"Stage makeup," says Houston in disgust. "Sure had me fooled."

Why would a First want to pass as a clone? I wonder.

Rizin wants an answer, too, and he orders the captain to

explain himself or suffer cruel consequences, which Rizin describes in horrible detail.

I'm sure the captain would rather die than deliver me up to a cyborg bounty hunter. I take the deepest breath and open the door to my hidden room. "Get your hands off him!"

"That's her, Uncle Li." Houston's expression is a mix of shock and glad-to-see-me.

Rizin drops the captain like a used towel and eyes me more carefully. "A clone worth a million dollars? Fascinating."

He examines my face the way someone would a dog or a horse. I jerk away and glare at Houston. How could I have ever thought I could trust a cyborg? "Rat!" I hiss.

I turn away in disgust. I take the captain's hand. "You okay?"

But the captain isn't pleased with my bravery. "Leanna, what were you thinking?" He is angry. "Why didn't you stay in your hiding place like you were told?"

"I wasn't going to let them hurt you." One look at the captain's face and I know I've acted without thinking . . . again. The hidden room wasn't built for my benefit. It was Captain Newton's special place — probably where he went to read books and transform himself into #9767. He'd let me use it so I'd be safe. Now I'd let strangers know about it. "So sorry," I whisper.

Rizin dismisses us all. "What's going on here?" he snaps at Captain Newton.

For the first time ever, the captain looks nervous. "I used the clone disguise so I could move freely among people, gathering information," he explains.

"What kind of information?" But before the captain can answer, Rizin snaps, "Don't play with me. Tell me the truth. Now!"

The captain never flinches. "I could find out things as a clone that a captain might not be able to. So I created a clone, gave it some fake papers, and the rest you know."

"But why?" Rizin insisted.

The captain wipes his face; more orange comes off. "A clone is not programmed to lie, steal, or cheat, so even though it's unorthodox, customers here on Gypsy City choose to conduct business with a Second rather than a First."

Rizin tilts his head in my direction. "What about her? Is she in disguise, too?"

"I was paid to get her from St. Louis to New Orleans." I thought it was Natchez. But I keep my mouth shut. The captain hurries on, as if he's more nervous than he really is. "That's all I know. Later, I learned from the news there's a bounty on her head. I knew people were going to try to get that million-dollar reward money, so —"

Rizin interrupts. "Who paid you to transport her?"

"It was all electronically transmitted. No legs or mouth attached."

Rizin seems to accept what the captain tells him, although it isn't the whole story. Clones may not have been programmed to lie, but the captain is a master.

I wonder if the captain is truly terrified of Rizin, or if he's pretending to be. I do see that he didn't need my help. I should have stayed put in my hideaway.

Rizin turns to me. "Come," he orders, snapping his fingers as though I am a dog. "Houston says you just found out you're a clone. Tell me what you know. Do you have a scrapbook? Files? Anything? I want them."

"I don't . . ."

"You're not altered like regular clones," Rizin says as he grabs for my commglasses. "I want to know more about you now!"

"All I know is Joe Spiller came to arrest my mother. Mom told me to run, and —"

Rizin's expression changes. "Go back," he shouts. "Joe Spiller came to arrest your mother?" Each of his words grows louder. Houston watches every move I make. I will myself not to show fear.

"Yes, he and his biobots came to our house," I answer, showing as much confidence as I can.

Rizin's hands ball into two fists. "So, they've got their top gun on the case." Rizin grips a small elephant figurine on the captain's desk. He squeezes it so tightly it's reduced to a handful of powder. "My old friend, Joe Spiller. I should have known."

"Uncle Li, you need to see this breaking news," says Houston, who points to the T. The announcer says, *Taylor Graham, the newly elected High Chancellor of The WFN, is preparing to speak to the people of the world.*

Graham's strongest supporters gather around him as the camera scans the group. Rizin bristles when he sees Spiller standing with the Chinese delegation. He swears under his breath. The sound of his voice is more chilling than before.

"Taylor Graham is about to begin his speech," says the news anchor. I watch with every muscle tight in my body.

Chancellor Graham begins:

"We are aware now that this subversive organization known as The Liberty Bell is not confined to the United States. This organization is worldwide and therefore a threat to our planet. The Liberty Bell is a group determined to disrupt our way of life and to destroy world economics. We have apprehended hundreds of these dissidents on the North American continent and more arrests are expected in Asia, Africa, and Europe, everywhere this group has infiltrated: businesses, schools, churches, and yes, even governments. Anyone coming forward with information will be rewarded handsomely. Don't be fooled. The Liberty Bell Movement usurps our most precious words, justice, liberty, and freedom, and uses them for their own dead-end ideology. But we are stronger than they are. We have right on our side. And that will give us the might to be victorious."

Rizin glares at me. "Not a word about you," he says. "Either Graham doesn't need you anymore, or he knows where you are! Was this program recorded or live?" he asks Houston.

"I think it was done earlier," Houston answers.

Rizin turns toward the door. "We need to get out of here. Now!"

But it is already too late.

"Look," shouts Houston, pointing at the security monitor. Joe Spiller and his biobots are boarding Gypsy City.

"Quick! This way," I say, rushing to the bathroom in my hiding place. "There's an exit here."

The captain closes the door behind us. We watch on the security monitor inside our hiding place as the biobots crash through the captain's office door. "They ain't here, boss," a biobot says to Spiller.

Next to Spiller is the farcar dealer who saw me in the captain's office a week ago. "Do I get the reward money?" he asks, and I realize he's the one who's turned me in, not Houston.

Spiller growls. "She's not captured yet."

We start for the overhead hatch that leads to the third level. The captain goes first. Then Houston. Li Rizin and I are to go next, but Rizin gestures for me to be still. One of the biobots is nearby.

We watch the security monitor as the biobots sniff and inspect everything. "Humans. Hmmm . . . Been here seconds ago." They scan the walls. "Titanium!"

Spiller searches frantically for a lead, some clue to help him find me. "Are you sure she was here?" Spiller asks.

"The captain sent her to sit in the hallway," the farcar dealer says, pointing to where he had seen me last.

Spiller grunts as he touches the wall where I'd stood and the floor where I'd sat with my knees pulled up to my chin. I remember being out-of-my-mind-crazy with fear. Rizin watches the monitor, and his body tenses up. He grits his teeth and releases a slow, menacing growl. Clearly, there is some bad history between him and Spiller. I sense how hard it is for Rizin to stop himself from smashing through the wall and attacking his enemy. To me, Rizin is just as scary as Spiller, but Rizin is helping me now. So he feels less threatening.

"They can't get off this junk heap," says one of the biobots. "We'll have her in custody within minutes. Won't we, boss?"

Spiller doesn't answer.

The search turns up no leads. Spiller and the biobots leave. The farcar dealer follows. He's still whining, "When did you say I get the money?"

I shimmy out of the hatch with Rizin behind me. We join the others and hurry down the third-level corridor. That's when I remember I've left my backpack. "I've got to go back," I say. "My backpack has all my things in it — my father's memory stick and my swifting gear. I can't leave them."

"Sorry, Leanna," says the captain. "We can't go back now."

I can accept the loss of everything except my father's memory stick. My insides tug me in opposite directions. I want my backpack, but I want freedom more. "Okay! Let's go," I say, losing one more part of my past.

No one knows the ins and outs of Gypsy City better than

Captain Newton. We make our way to the garage, where the farcars and cargo planes are parked like ducks on a pond. Spiller has posted Clone Humane Society troops at all exit doors. "They're only armed with shocker rods, so they don't want to kill you," says Houston.

This is the first Houston has spoken to me since he's come back to Gypsy City. I'm so angry I can't even look at him.

The captain paces. "Li Rizin," he says, "I'm in a very hard spot right now. I need help to get Leanna off this barge."

"At first it was about the bounty," says Rizin. "But now it's become a personal thing. If Spiller wants Leanna, then I'll die keeping him and whoever he's working for from getting their hands on her. No matter what it takes."

"Count me in, too," says Houston.

I can't believe what I'm hearing. "No, Captain Newton," I say.

The captain steps past me and continues talking to Rizin. "You must understand, Rizin, that you and Houston helping us will be misinterpreted. It will appear as though you're members of The Liberty Bell, an enemy of the Federation."

Rizin speaks with a slow, sure tone. "I couldn't care less about your organization, with all its talk about justice and rights — my concern is Spiller."

The captain explains quickly. "Leanna, I am putting your safety in the hands of Rizin and Houston."

I cross my arms and take a stand. "Not gonna happen," I say. "Don't I have something to say about all this? I'm not a stupid clone!" As soon as the words are out of my mouth, I want to disown them. But I don't stop. "Okay, so I *am* a clone, and Li Rizin and his sidekick have come to turn me in for the bounty. Who says they won't finish the job as soon as they get a chance?" I take a breath, but I have more to say. "Please don't forget, Captain Newton, Rizin almost beat you to death a few minutes ago. Now you're going to put *my* life in *his* hands? I don't think so. I'll take my chances on my own. Thank you very much, but no thank you!"

"I don't envy you," says Captain Newton with a soft chuckle.

Rizin gives me a scary scowl, and Houston shakes his head in agreement. Then it's as if I'd never spoken. The captain puts his plan into motion. "Take her," he says.

He tells Houston to lead us to the exhaust system in engineering. "I'll meet you under Gypsy City with a farcar in ten minutes." The captain and Rizin set the time on their commglasses, then the captain rushes back to his quarters.

Houston takes us down the steps to engineering. We find the air exhaust vent and climb into it. We wait.

Soon the biobots come rumbling into engineering, destroying everything. They sniff but find nothing.

"Did you check the exhaust vent?" one of them asks the other.

"No, junkhead," answers the second biobot. "Escapees only hide in exhaust vents in the movies. Nobody would be dense enough to hide in such an obvious place."

"And we're not going to be stupid enough to look," says the first biobot.

They belch and head toward the door, bumping together as they try to pass through the opening at the same time. *You're the dumb ones*, I say silently to myself.

Li Rizin's commglasses beep, signaling that it's time for us to slide. The slope of the vent is steep, and there will be no stopping once we begin our escape. Rizin goes first, followed by Houston. Then I let go, sailing out of the vent. Rizin catches my arm with one powerful hand. Captain Newton isn't there waiting for us!

The three of us dangle hundreds of feet above the Mississippi River, swinging like loose rigging. The only thing that keeps us from plunging to our deaths in the muddy water below is this cyborg's powerful bionic arms. With one hand, he's holding on to a piece of metal sticking out from the vent; with the other he's holding me. Houston is clinging to Rizin's waist. The metal moans under our weight.

"Hold tight," Rizin says.

Just then, we see a fartruck jet out of the parking dock and head for us. Within seconds, the captain, disguised again as #9767, is hovering below the vent, and one by one we jump into the fartruck.

Spiller is aware of our escape now. He switches on the outside speakers. "You corrupted Second! I order you to come back! I'm going to personally decommission you!"

"Did Spiller see who we are?" I ask.

"Excuse my grammar, but in the words of a corrupted clone, Spiller saw *I*," says the captain, laughing as he speeds us away.

The captain lands the fartruck on Atlantis, a self-sufficient, weapon-free, research biosphere located at Ibo Landing off the coast of Georgia. The only way in is through a dome that opens at scheduled intervals. We have just missed an opening, so we wait for the next one.

Atlantis is like no other place in the world, and I am anxious to see it. No V-program can capture the feel of what it's like to fly over Atlantis.

Houston explains that Atlantis is completely man-made, a floating island about the size of Washington, DC. I know all of this, but I let Houston explain it to me anyway. "The covered dome is made of titanium and reinforced with wafer-thin clear steel," he says.

"A lot of research goes on here, right?" I ask.

"Our whole space program is housed on Atlantis," says Houston.

It feels good to be talking to Houston again, even if it's only about steel and titanium.

When we land, we're met by Zion Milner, who explains that he is my porter. He is a low-ranking manager of the university housing department. According to plan, Zion has registered us in a university guest dormitory, a huge complex shaped in the form of stacked L's.

It's odd, being here at Atlantis University, the location of the David Montgomery International Biotech Research and Development Center, which is funded by the Topas Corporation. The corporation has a lot of nerve naming their biotech lab in honor of my great-grandfather, especially after they've done so much to destroy his work.

Li Rizin is checking out the landscape. "Smart move," he says, nodding his approval. "They'll never think we've come here."

"Like a mouse hiding in the lion's ear," says Zion.

Zion's nothing like the captain, who is strict but kind. Zion is businesslike and totally humorless.

We sip blackberry tea while Zion puts our papers in order. The tea is soothing as I listen to the captain explain how he got past Spiller. "Disguised as my clone," he begins, "I told the guards that I'd been instructed by my First to make a medical emergency delivery."

"Did the guards question you?" Houston asks.

"Sure they did. They asked if I'd seen Leanna, and I told them I knew nothing. The guards let me go because . . ."

". . . clones can't lie," we say in unison.

Zion leads us to our rooms through the corridors of Holmiester Hall. "Atlantis is known for its luxury facilities and fine food," he explains, but quickly he adds, "your rooms, however, are notably average and so is the food. It isn't gourmet, but it's nourishing."

I can't help but ask, "Is there a reason why we don't get luxury?"

Zion explains. "If we put you up in luxury, it will make people wonder who you are. As your porter, I must insist that you keep a very low profile here at Atlantis."

What Zion calls average is much nicer than I expected. My room is large, with a big window overlooking a garden. After being on Gypsy City, this place *is* a luxury to me.

"I've stayed in worse," says Houston, looking around.

Zion then shows Houston to his quarters and takes the captain to a private area where he can remove his clone disguise. After a quick meal, the captain comes to my room to say good-bye.

"Might you be needing this, Miss Ma'am?" he asks, speaking as #9767. He hands me my backpack! Everything's inside, including Daddy's memory stick. "I found the backpack when I went back to my office."

Words don't come to me. All I can do is hug the captain.

We walk out onto the balcony. "What if Spiller tracks us here?" I ask.

The captain replies, "I jammed all communications that operate the docking doors so they couldn't follow."

"What will you do now? It's too dangerous to go back."

"As Captain Newton I *can* return. Everybody saw my dysfunctional clone go out of control. And they saw #9767 help you escape."

"But how will you get back on board?" I ask.

"Gypsy City is my vessel. I know every inch of it," the captain says with a wink and a nod. "When it's dark, I'll sneak back on board and hide myself where my villainous clone put me." He gives a little chuckle. "Of course, I'll rant and rave and promise to have my clone decommissioned . . . when I catch him. And in time I'll get another clone," he says, smiling.

I know it is time for the captain to go. I hug him again, tighter this time. "What am I going to do without you and #9767 to look after me? I'll miss you both."

"Zion, Rizin, and Houston will take good care of you." There's a quaver in the captain's voice. "My work is done."

"I don't want you to go," I say softly.

"There is still much to do in The Movement, Leanna. Promise me that you'll use your brain. Think. Take your time. Plan ahead. Watch. Listen." The captain gently touches my cheek.

"I will," I whisper. "I'm going to miss you."

"I'll miss you, too. And that's no lie."

Then he is gone.

I'm not sure how long I'm to stay at Atlantis. Zion asks to meet in his office. Breakfast waits for us when we arrive.

Right away I feel something's wrong. "Leanna." Zion clears his throat. "I've decided it would be wise for you to disguise yourself as a clone."

"How come? I'm already a clone. Why do I need to disguise myself?"

"Must you question everything?" Rizin says.

Zion tries to reason with me. "The Federation will be looking for a girl who doesn't resemble a clone. You need to look like what they don't expect."

"No," I say, backing up to the door. "There's got to be a better way to stay safe."

"We can do this easily and be done with it, or *you* can choose the hard way, but it will still get done," warns Zion, who looks to Rizin for help.

I try to run, but Rizin catches me. No amount of struggling or begging can change their minds.

"Okay," I say at last, accepting defeat. "You can make me do it, but you can't make me like it!"

Zion applies purple stage makeup on me.

"The color for academic clones," Houston says. "They usually are a little smarter than domestic clones."

"Don't talk to me," I snap. "I hate you both for doing this."

Next come hair shears cold against my scalp. I fight to break free, but there is no release from Rizin's cyborg grip. I watch my dark hair fall to the floor. I am soon bald. Next, my eyebrows are shaven off. Zion dabs the purple onto all my bald places.

"Don't get near any heavy-duty cleaning fluid, or you're busted," says Rizin, standing back to admire me. "And use gloves when you work with water."

Although there is logic in their decision, I hate the way I look. But I can now go unnoticed. I am a clone who looks like a clone, not a human.

Rizin insists that I stay out of the way of people and that I speak as little as possible to anyone on Atlantis. "You may look like a clone, but you don't act like one," he says. "Just find a comfortable spot, be still, and . . ."

". . . don't call attention to yourself," I say, recalling #9767's words.

"She needs a clone number," says Houston.

I shoot Houston a look that could strangle. "What about #1010?" he says, trying not to laugh at me.

"I hate you," I hiss.

Rizin nods. "#1010. Sounds good."

#1010!

"My name is Leanna!" I scream. "I will *never* answer to #1010. Never."

"Okay," Zion says, holding up his hands as a shield, "you'll be #1010 only when we're out in public."

As upset as I am, I soon see that as #1010 I can move about freely. I can listen and learn, just as #9767 did on board Gypsy City.

Later that day, Zion stops by my room to bring me a sandwich. "Have you heard anything about my mom?" I ask.

"No, but I did hear from Captain Newton," Zion says. "He sends his regards. The captain made it back to Gypsy City and slipped on board just as he said he would. Everything was blamed on #9767, who is now missing."

Zion leaves as Houston comes in.

"Just checking," he says.

I lift the bread on the sandwich and find out it's made of Agu, a new protein substitute, supposedly high in nutrients. "I don't eat imaginary meat." I push it away.

"I do," Houston says, taking my sandwich. "It's good with mustard."

I frown. "Nasty!"

"Who's nasty? Me or the sandwich?" he asks. "Are you still mad at me?"

"Being nice won't work, Houston." I hold him in my gaze. "Tell the truth. You *were* going to turn me in for the money!"

"I knew you'd think that, but it's not how it happened," he says, declaring himself innocent. Although I'm sure it was the farcar dealer who turned me in, I don't fully believe Houston, either.

"Listen, I called Uncle Li to ask if a clone could look and act like you. Before I knew it, he was on board Gypsy City with me, pinning me to the wall. You know what he's like when he wants information. I had to tell him what I know. Besides, if you'll recall, you asked me to help you."

"And you said no."

"Well, I changed my mind."

"You're just as mean as your uncle, and I don't want any more to do with you than I have to. So . . ." I dismiss him with a flip of my hand. "See you."

"The appreciation you showed us for all we've done for you was so heartfelt," he says sarcastically.

But I'm too tired, even for Houston's attitude. I answer simply and honestly. "You're right. I apologize for not saying thank you for helping me get to safety."

Houston is caught off guard. He wants me to argue with him. I can see it in his eyes. Then he softens.

"Okay. Truce. False start. Let's begin again." He stands up and extends his hand. "I'm Houston Ye. I'm a cyborg. And you?"

"I sure need a friend. Even a cyborg will do," I say with a half smile. "Like you need a clone for a friend, right?" I say, laughing.

"Forgiven?" he asks.

"Call me #1010 again and I'll . . ."

"Hey, let's go explore Atlantis."

Houston has been to Atlantis many times. Scientists, architects, engineers, social scientists, and psychologists from all over the world designed and built the biosphere, known as the Domed City, twenty years ago as the model of a future space station on a planet with an environment hostile to humankind.

Houston explains that thousands of computers generating millions of holographic projections create the perfect atmosphere with wind, birds, clouds, and a magnificent sun that is stripped of its harmful rays.

One step out of Holmiester Hall and I am quickly reminded that I'm a clone. I am expected to walk a step behind Houston with my head down. I agree to do it because it feels so good to be outside. I take a deep breath. Atlantis is so much cleaner and smells so much better than Gypsy City. It is weapon-free and crime-free, and since no one locks anything, entry cards are a thing of the past.

"I feel a breeze on my face," I say, smiling.

"There's even a simulated ocean that has sandy beaches with seagulls."

The streets are narrow but connected on many levels. To create the illusion of space, the planners of Atlantis have used mirrors and glass. "Shoppers can see streets and people on four levels, much like the shops in the malls of the late twentieth century," Houston says, as awed as I am.

I've never seen anything like this before. I stand in the middle of the boulevard and turn around and around, taking it all in.

"Crazy clone," a shopper says, pushing me out of the way.

"Where's your First?"

"Come on #1010," Houston says, grabbing my arm. "And take that too-proud look off your face."

When we're away from the shoppers, Houston reminds me that part of my disguise is for me to *act* like a clone. "Clones don't challenge Firsts. You know this. If you don't want to be locked in your room, then stay under control."

"I hate the idea of having to be subservient to people whose blood is red just like mine." I start to storm away.

"You'd better start acting like a clone or you're going to get in serious trouble."

I know Houston is right, so I lower my head, drop back, and walk two steps behind him.

"This isn't easy," he says. "But hang in there."

The next day, Houston and I get an early start in our exploration of Atlantis. "We're going to a place that is totally galactic," he says.

We make our way through the biosphere until we reach a

level that leads to a huge stadium. I gasp because we're at the Atlantis University vs. the University of Iowa championship swifting game. I'd forgotten about the big event, but now it's moments away.

It couldn't be a more perfect day. There isn't even an artificial cloud in the sky. The morning's sun warms my body. The two best teams in the league are facing each other for the play-offs. "How did you get tickets?" I whisper. "Steal 'em?"

"Uncle Li got them."

"*He* steal 'em?"

"No. He bought them for you."

"He didn't. That's so not Rizin."

"Well, he got them for *us*," Houston says.

I shake my head, still not believing him.

"Okay," Houston finally admits, "Uncle Li had to go back to the Moon base, so he gave these tickets to me."

"Why'd you lie?" I ask.

Houston shrugs. "I want you to think better of my uncle Li. He's really not so bad."

"Really?" I decide not to say more. I'm going to see my champion, Cy Dennis, play in the game of games, and this is enough talk for now.

Houston hands me my ticket and points to where my seat is located. "Aren't you coming with me?" I ask.

"No. I have to sit in the cyborg section and you have to sit with the clones. Meet you here at Gate 12 afterward."

By the time I climb to the fifth tier of the stadium, the swifting chamber looks like a toy box. The best way to see the players is on the big screens set up throughout the stadium. If

I'd wanted to see the game on a monitor, I could have stayed in my room and watched it on the T. But I'm getting to see Cy Dennis live, which is awesome no matter how many tiers I have to climb.

Instead of the one-on-one matches I'm used to, the college teams are made up of nine players each. All nine players on each team enter the chamber; only three players compete per match. The winners of three out of five matches win the trophy and bragging rights. Of course, Iowa is my favorite, but all the clones around me are cheering for Atlantis. I play it safe and cheer with the crowd.

"So you like the Atlantis team?" I ask a blue clone sitting next to me.

"My First says to cheer for Atlantis," the blue clone answers.

I want to shout that I'm an Iowa supporter, but I don't.

The game is close, with Atlantis answering every Iowa point. Iowa can put it to bed, but a player misses the toss. Atlantis scores, taking the game to the fifth and final match. With the score two to two, the winning players float to the center of the chamber. Their teammates cling to the side of the chamber in their harnesses to keep from floating into play.

Cy Dennis is known for her accuracy at the point wall. I want to cheer for her, but I will call attention to myself if I do.

Franklin Epps, the Atlantis senior called the Bubble Master, is the best defender in the National College Swifting Association, the NCSA league. The pros have been talking to Epps since he was a freshman.

When the bubble is released, the cheering and shouting are deafening. A sea of orange, purple, blue, and red clones shout, "Go, Atlantis Bumblebees!" They all wave black-and-yellow flags. I get caught up in the excitement and start chanting, too, even though my heart is with Iowa and Cy. It's so hard to keep my true feelings buried. Who can? No wonder Topas has to insert chips in the clones to make them accept nonsense like this. I don't like this clone life.

Point for point, it's a hard-fought match. Cy makes the final point using her famous flip-and-spin move, and I want to shout. When the game is over, the trophy is on its way to Iowa. I smile on the inside.

On my way to meet Houston at Gate 12, I take a wrong turn and end up in a restricted area. I run right into a Clone Humane Society officer.

"What are you doing back here, Second?"

I keep my head down and cower. "Lost, sir. Need help finding Gate 12." The hardest part is remembering not to use *I*.

The officer studies me closely. "Your number?"

"1010, sir."

The officer checks out my papers on his computer. "Property of the university," he says. Everything seems to be in order, thanks to Zion.

"Get out of here," the officer commands.

As I walk away, I hear the officer tell his partner, "They say the purple ones have more sense then the others, but you could have fooled me."

I finally reach Gate 12, and Houston is relieved. "I was getting worried. What happened?"

I tell him the whole story as we walk to the top of a hill overlooking the bay, where small boats bob on the holographic ocean. I'm still excited about the game. Houston and I share ideas about a few of the referees' calls, the great moves by the swifters, and the last point, when Cy did a corkscrew spin and flipped the bubble over Epps's shoulder for the winning thirty-pointer. "Amazing game," I say. "Thank your uncle for the ticket."

We sit quietly in the grass. "We're in a painting from the late twenty-first century," I say, smiling. "So realistic."

If I could make a memory stick of this day, I'd save my feelings about the game and about sitting on this hill with a friend.

"Atlantis is a prototype for space stations that will eventually be built on the Moon and Mars and beyond," Houston comments. "I'd love to be a part of the space program. Go out there, beyond what we know. But that's crazy to even think about."

"No, it isn't," I say. "You're just as capable as anyone."

"Leanna, I'm a cyborg, remember? There are laws that limit us. I'm passing right now because I can, but many of my cyborg brothers *can't* hide. They get mistreated in ways you can't imagine."

I tighten my fists. "The laws are wrong and they will be changed!"

Houston and I are fringing. You'd never know it the way we act. He stops at a sidewalk vendor, where he buys a bottle of Viti-fluid, a new drink on the market made from filtered seawater fortified with vitamins. I watch Houston drink. "Clones eat by themselves. I'll buy you one to drink later," he whispers.

Houston finds a bench in a lovely rose garden. I have to sit on the ground, but I still enjoy the beautiful flowers. We sit quietly, watching Firsts and their clones.

I am particularly interested in the clones that are my color. "What do purple clones do?" I ask Houston.

"Most purples are academic assistants who work in education from preschool through graduate school, just helping out. You're at the cutoff age for clone production, so they'd probably use you for working with very young children and animals," he explains.

A silver clone passes. I've never seen one before. "What kind is that?"

"A designer model. Probably belongs to a movie star or pro swifter. They cost six million dollars or more."

A purple clone and a First teacher bring a group of

preschoolers to the park for playtime. Houston is in a good mood so I figure it's the right time to find out some things without sounding too curious. "Is Rizin really your uncle? You don't look like family."

Houston takes a gulp of Viti-fluid. "Most people think so. But no, he isn't my real uncle, not really."

"What does 'not really' mean? Either he is or he isn't your uncle."

"Not genetically. Uncle Li and my father were best friends in the Federation Special Forces. Joe Spiller and Taylor Graham were also part of their group."

I can tell Houston wants to talk. Something has opened up between us.

"Uncle Li's lasercopter was shot down in the Niger River Bend in West Africa during the Last War. When he woke up from his coma, most of his body had been replaced with bionic parts. Word is, there isn't an original organ in his body, except his brain. It took seventeen operations in ten years to rebuild him.

"Once Uncle Li had lost his humanity and was declared a cyborg, Spiller and Graham stopped visiting and soon had nothing to do with him. This is why Uncle Li resents Spiller so much.

"But Dad stuck with Uncle Li through the long years of rehab. And Uncle Li never forgot Dad's loyalty, especially when my accident happened and I ended up being a cyborg, too. Uncle Li helped with my rehab every hard step of the way. He's a tough character, and as far as I'm concerned, he's one hundred percent friend. You couldn't ask for a better person to be on your side."

Knowing this about Rizin made him less scary. "Where's your Dad now?" I ask.

"Dead."

"Mine, too," I say.

I want to tell Houston more of my story. And I want to hear more of his, but we are interrupted by a scream.

The purple clone who is chaperoning the little kids is struggling to get them to safety. The brakes on a food vendor's cart have failed, and the cart is heading straight for the crowd of children crossing the street!

Without a moment's hesitation, the clone steps in front of the cart and takes a full frontal blow! The First teacher rushes the students to safety, while the purple clone lies on the ground, crushed by the cart. No one comes to help her.

"Please! Someone, over here," I shout.

Houston covers my mouth and yanks me away. Now I scream and struggle to free myself. "Get off me! That clone is hurt and nobody cares!"

"Leanna, stop! Think! You can't help without jeopardizing your own safety."

"I never knew how awful . . ." I say, unable to finish what I'm thinking. That could be me lying under the cart. "What's going to happen to her?" I bite down on my lip.

"Members of the Clone Humane Society are the only ones who are allowed to make the decision to treat or decommission an injured clone."

The harsh reality of clone existence is a shadow always follow-ing me. They let that purple clone lie there like she was a disposable towel. Useless. I have been ignorant of how clones and cyborgs are treated, but now I want to do something about it.

I check in with my Custodians. "Ah, here we are together again," says Ben Franklin. He looks at me carefully. "My, my, how different you appear."

"My porters think it is best to disguise me as a clone."

"Grotesque," scoffs my great-grandfather with a grunt. "Look how they exploit my work. There's no need for clones to look the way they do. Not even for profit's sake."

I explain what happened in the park with the purple clone. "I understand why Mom and Doc Doc became members of The Liberty Bell. I want it to be official. I am a Bell Ringer, too!"

"Bravo," cheers my great-grandfather. "Now, that's a chip off the old wagon."

"Block," corrects Mrs. Roosevelt. "My dear, you don't need to join. Just do your part," she says.

My great-grandfather applauds. "You are going to blow the Topas Corporation right out of the sink."

"When will you get those old sayings right?" asks Mrs. Roosevelt with a smile. "It's out of the water!"

"Water. Sink. No matter," says my great-grandfather. "The Topas Corporation is going down the drain." He touches my face. "Just look at my great-granddaughter," he says. "She's as pretty as her mother."

"Now that you are a member, let us share our complete history with you," says Justice Harlan.

I spend the next few days talking with my Custodians and sharing Doc Doc's scrapbook about The Liberty Bell.

My life has not gotten back to normal. Even though I've managed to settle into Atlantis these past few weeks, I still miss Mom and worry about her and Doc Doc more than I let on.

Zion has gotten Houston a job as a shuttle driver, so we don't see each other too much during the day.

Various departments rent workers from the university clone pool. Zion got me assigned to the hospital. I love working with the babies. It reminds me of Doc Doc's clinic. I made friends with a family whose infant son is having a reaction to his diabetes vaccination. One out of every thousand children has reactions from mild to severe. Little Micah's is severe, almost life threatening.

"You are so compassionate and loving," says Micah's mother.

"He's so little and helpless," I say.

"Thank you for taking care of him. He is precious to us."

"All life is precious."

Micah's mother looks at me suspiciously. "#1010, that's an advanced idea for a clone."

I try to look clueless, but she stares at me harder.

"There's a lot of talk about a breed of clones that is being created to take over the world," she says. Then she sighs as if dismissing the thought. "Perhaps I'm a little on edge."

She takes baby Micah home, and I never see him or his mother again.

When I tell Zion the story, he decides it's best to place me in the research lab, where I work only with animals. My new boss gives me the most mindless job imaginable.

I'm put in a room filled with gray-colored rocks all different sizes and shapes. There seems to be several hundred of them, all neatly lined up row by row in long, shallow boxes filled with sand. The room is dimly lit and very hot. My task is to turn the rocks over twice a day and water them once a day. Are these the rocks the custodians mentioned, I wonder. When I explain it all to Houston, he jokingly says I am a rock star. This sounds too much like a clone joke, so I refuse to laugh.

One evening after Houston gets off from his job as a shuttle driver, he comes to the lab and we go fringing. We walk back to the dorm, me following behind him as any dutiful clone should. "Has your stone garden bloomed yet?" he asks when we get to the dorm.

But I'm not up for joking. "Do you know about The Liberty Bell Movement?" I ask suddenly.

"Well, yeah, but not too much," he says. "You're a part of it, right? And I'm helping you, so that means I'm a part of it, too, I guess."

I nod. "I officially became a Bell Ringer. Let me tell you

what we stand for. Then maybe you might want to formally join us."

Houston is listening carefully. He doesn't respond, but he seems interested. We spend the rest of the evening talking about The Movement and what it would mean for both of us.

Over time I learn my way around the complex that is named after my great-grandfather. Clones can't eat together according to code, so most of the time I look for a quiet place to have lunch. Today I find a huge aircraft hangar. Inside is a large spaceship. The hangar doors are open, so I cautiously walk up the ramp to look in the window of the craft. The doors open suddenly. I step inside what appears to be the command center. The door shuts as easily as it opens.

"Hello?" comes a voice.

"Who's there?" I call out.

"I am RUBy," says a young girl's voice coming from a screen stretched across the front of the command center. "Over here," the voice says. This girl is a computer, but not like any I've ever seen.

"What are you?" I ask.

RUBy responds, "I am a prototype of a galaxy-class spaceship made of Rythonium, Uranius 2He, and Byolythy. My name is an acronym of those words — R-U-By."

"Are you the ship?"

"Not exactly," RUBy answers. "I operate the ship."

"You are the computer?" I try to figure it out.

"I've been programmed," she says.

I'm suddenly afraid of getting caught in this unfamiliar place. "I have to go," I say. The doors open, and I hurry away.

"Come see me again," RUBy calls.

Houston doesn't believe me when I tell him about RUBy. "It's a giant spacecraft big enough to carry a hundred people or more," I describe. "And it's all computer powered."

"You're telling me you just wandered into a hangar that housed a galaxy-class spaceship that talks? They just left the door open for anybody to walk in?"

It does sound silly, but it's true. "This is Atlantis. Who could steal it? They couldn't get past the fly-out." Excitement builds as I talk. "It's huge."

"So you say."

The next day, Houston meets me at the lab at noon so I can show him the hangar. The doors slide open and Houston and I step on board.

"RUBy," I call when we get inside.

As soon as Houston sees RUBy the ship, he's speechless. "This is unbelievable." Houston's eyes are wide.

"See, I told you. Now let's go before we get caught."

But it's too late.

A kid who looks a little younger than I am comes charging into the hangar. He seems confused and angry.

"Get out of here!" he demands. "Open the door, RUBy. Now."

The doors slide open. The kid rushes in. "Have they done

something to damage you, RUBy?" He pushes me out of the way to get to the screen.

I know better than to say anything more. Houston speaks up fast.

"I'm Houston Ye." He goes to shake the kid's hand. The kid lets Houston's hand hang in the air.

"I'm Carlos Pace."

"Are you related to Dr. Marcus Pace, the world-renowned astro-engineer?" Houston asks.

Carlos doesn't answer. "Who are you? Why are you and a clone in here?" he snaps.

"We accidentally wandered into this hangar. It wasn't locked, so we came in and found RUBy," Houston tries to explain.

"Get out of here," Carlos demands. "I don't have time for you." He turns to RUBy and puts his hand on her screen. He starts in with things we don't understand. "He knows. I gave him the proof, but he still won't change his mind. They are planning to go ahead with it. I tried so hard to talk him out of it."

"You did what you could. I thank you," RUBy says.

I don't know what all this means, but I can feel the emotion in Carlos.

Then Carlos remembers we're still here. "Didn't I tell you to get out of here?"

"RUBy has to open the doors," Houston says quietly.

Carlos lowers his voice. "I'm not going to turn you in, but don't ever come back here again or I'll call security.

We've never had to lock up before, but I guess we'll have to start."

The doors open and we leave.

"I feel them," says RUBy.

Carlos calls us back. "RUBy likes you. That means there's something special about the two of you. If you want to visit again, I'll get you clearance."

Houston is quick to answer. "What about tomorrow?"

For the rest of the week, Carlos and Houston eat lunch together and talk endlessly about spaceships, black holes, and space mining. As a clone, I'm expected to eat separately. Carlos and Houston go to a far-off corner to share theories about fuels. I use this as my chance to get to know RUBy better. I notice that RUBy's screen goes from blue to red.

"Why did your screen color change, RUBy?" I ask.

RUBy explains that when the panel is blue, she's at rest, quiet, listening.

"You're red now. What does that mean?" I ask.

"Joy. Happy. I'm happy to see Carlos and Houston and you."

"How can a computer feel emotions?" I want to know.

"Carlos programmed me this way." RUBy's screen dims a bit.

"Sorry to ask so many questions."

RUBy says, "I have a question for you. Are you a new generation of clone?"

"Why do you ask?" I say, feeling myself go red, too, not from being happy but from the warm flush that comes when fear strikes.

RUBy says, "You scan as a clone, but you don't have chips or brain implants. And I'm picking up second-generation cells from you."

Am I busted? "Clones don't know stuff like that," I say, turning another question to RUBy. "Why did they program such a big ship with the voice of a young girl?"

"Carlos helped program the command center. This voice was supposed to be temporary, but he never got around to changing it."

"Is Carlos some kind of genius?"

"He is," says RUBy. "But he's also a very lonely boy. He needs a human friend."

"Aren't you his friend?"

"Yes, friend."

"Can we be friends?" I ask.

RUBy's screen turns bright red. She giggles like a little girl, and the whole ship shakes.

It is soon time for us to return to our afternoon chores. "I have to go turn the rocks," I say.

"What rocks?" asks RUBy.

I tell her about my job.

RUBy doesn't answer. Her starlight communication system activates, and she begins transmitting.

Carlos comes quick. "RUBy, what are you doing?"

"I have been left no choice." RUBy's screen turns gray and shuts down suddenly.

I go back to work. I am busy turning my rocks when they start glowing like jewels in the sunlight. Small, medium, and large ones are alive with color. Some blink red. Others flash quick bursts of green that fade into yellow, then turn to green again. A row of rocks glows in a river of blue, from light aqua to deep blue-black. The rocks are beautiful and fascinating.

I watch them, and I feel a presence. I prepare to explain to a First that I have done nothing to make the rocks act so strangely. "Who's there?" I call.

Two dark figures step out of the shadows. All the rocks begin flashing yellow, as if they're *talking* to the strangers. I am about to run but stop when the figures speak.

"We mean you no harm," they say as one. "Our kind are everywhere. We watch and observe and try to keep order in our world, our sector of the Universe. We are The O."

"So you *do* exist." I sense what they will say next. I am listening so carefully.

"We come with a warning and a message," The O begin. "The message is this: In 2171, humankind will have mastered the technology necessary for intergalactic space travel. Unfortunately, from what we see in the future, you are not ready. Heed our warning: Unless all life-forms are free on your planet, we will have no choice but to stop you. You must become a Custodian of your world."

"Benjamin Franklin thought it was witchcraft that brought you to him," I say.

"There is no sorcery involved. We are appearing to Benjamin Franklin in 1787, to Justice John Marshall Harlan in 1896, to First Lady Eleanor Roosevelt in 1943, to Dr. David Montgomery in 2088, and to you in 2170, all at the same time."

"I'm the nameless girl," I shout. "It's me!"

The O continue, telling of pasts, presents, and futures that stretch into infinity.

"Spherical time!" I say. "Time that runs in a circle."

The O keep on. "Liberty, freedom, and justice are not easy for young civilizations to achieve. So we step into Earth's history when ideas such as freedom and justice are attainable goals. We hope you will start a new ribbon that will lead to a different future than we see — a better one."

"So I am the last Custodian!"

"Yes."

"What am I supposed to do?"

The O don't answer this time.

The rocks become a light show of colors, flashing and blinking. The O see me watching them and say, "They are not rocks."

Mrs. Roosevelt and the other Custodians appear. I tell

them, "I am the last Custodian. And I know what they're talking about when they say, 'They are not rocks'!"

"That does not compute," says Mrs. Roosevelt. The others look puzzled, and I soon realize why.

Doc Doc didn't know how to program these guardians with information about me being the last Custodian or the meaning of the rocks. I reword my questions.

"Friends," I ask, "what is the girl with no name expected to do when she becomes a Custodian?"

Ben Franklin is, as usual, scientific in his approach to problem solving. Mrs. Roosevelt is all heart. Justice Harlan relies upon the law to right most wrongs, and my beloved great-grandfather is more optimistic than anyone I know.

"She will need to know how to communicate," says Franklin. "Just continue working for freedom and justice for all."

Mrs. Roosevelt pats me on the back of my hand. "She must remember to carry the torch forward. The O chose each one of us for a reason. So she must find that reason, then be brave. Work smart. Take heart."

"Leanna," Justice Harlan says, "how do you eat an elephant?"

"I don't know." I'm confused by the question.

"One bite at a time," the justice says with a slight chuckle.

"Huh?" I say with a blank face.

Justice Harlan explains. "What the Bell Ringers have accomplished in nearly four hundred years has been to eat an elephant too big for any one person to take on. When our time came, each one of us did what we could to move the cause forward. When the time comes, the last Custodian will take a bite out of the elephant. That means she will set our great cause ahead bit by bit."

Dr. Montgomery raises a finger. "She needs to know she will not be alone. There is a network surrounding her."

"Thank you," I say, hugging him. "May I call you Pap-Pap?"

"Of course," he says, his face beaming.

Rizin has contacted Houston. Things are going well at the Moon mining colony. Meanwhile, we are still on Atlantis, waiting to hear about Mom and Dr. Ayala's case. A court date has been set for December 18, 2170, just a week away, so I seek out Justice Harlan for advice.

"Mom's court case is coming up," I tell him. "I thought it would take much longer."

Justice Harlan explains. "Lawyers can petition the court through what is called an *extraordinary writ*. It asks the court to bypass the normal procedures and go straight to the front of the line."

"Do I have to go?" I ask.

"Yes, Leanna. You are The Liberty Bell defendants' best defense. You are proof that our cause is just. The other day you asked what a Custodian does. This is it — standing strong for a cause. This is what you must do as a leader. This is your bite out of the elephant!"

"I've never been in a courtroom. Not even a virtual one. What should I expect?" I want to know. There is blood rushing to my face.

Justice Harlan rubs his chin before answering. "I don't know these judges, but during my time on the Supreme Court, in the late 1800s, we asked questions to gather facts to support our opinions. May I suggest you give brief answers? Be poised, and above all, be honest."

"You've been so helpful, Justice Harlan," I say before leaving his presence.

I know that I am about to do something terrifying but very important. The O think I can do it. They've made me a Custodian, so like a good swifter, I'll take the bubble and try to score!

Zion wakes me at eight o'clock sharp. "Today is the day we've been waiting for, Leanna."

Houston explains. "According to the stringer on the T, your hologram will be sent to the Court at noon. Billions of people are going to be watching this."

"Thanks for letting me know that the world will see me, Houston. Now everybody will know that I'm a clone!"

I think about Sandra, and I feel like a traitor for being afraid to tell her the truth about me. Now that fear is being realized anyway.

Zion agrees that I shouldn't wear my clone disguise. He gets some cleaning liquid to take off the purple. I love uncovering myself after months of being colored. Zion also finds a wig that looks like my own hair, and he glues on eyebrows. To finish, I put on a clean pair of pants and a frisk top. I look like Leanna Deberry again, and it feels good.

When the time comes, I place the call with a set of untraceable commglasses. Right away, I am in the United States Supreme Court.

Mom and Doc Doc are standing outside the courtroom. I can't believe how my mother looks. Her face is so ashen. Dark circles ring her eyes. Her bottom lip twitches, and her hands move nervously. She looks like old photos of twentieth-century drug addicts. "Mom! Are you okay?" I shout.

Suddenly, the door slams shut. A United States Federal Marshal and another person appear. "So you've joined us," the man with the marshal says to me. "I'm Mr. Lyle Adams, attorney for the defendants. You are going to be our primary evidence," he says briskly. "Just answer the questions. Don't say a word about anything unless you are asked. And don't try to move outside your allotted space. Do you understand? No outbursts. And no more calling out to your mother."

"And you're supposed to be on our side?" I say.

I keep looking over at Mom. I try hard not to shout out to her. She never takes her eyes off me, either, and without her saying a word, I read her expression. *I'm so glad to see you. I'm okay. Don't worry. Do your best. Everything will be all right.*

Doc Doc looks much older and also very tired. And he's so much thinner now. His suit hangs on him like it was borrowed from a bigger man. He manages to keep his dignity, though. His head is held high.

The chief marshal bangs his gavel on the desk and announces, "The Honorable Chief Justice Granbury and the Associate Justices of the Supreme Court of the United States."

Everyone stands. All nine of the Supreme Court justices enter single file from a side door. Each takes his or her seat on the bench where an identifying placard is placed. There are monitor screens placed throughout the courtroom, where I watch the justices and where they can view me.

"Oyez! Oyez! Oyez!" calls the marshal. "All persons having business before the Honorable Supreme Court of the United States are admonished to draw near and give attention, for the Court is now sitting. God save the United States and this Honorable Court!"

"You may be seated," begins Chief Justice John Granbury, who is in the center chair. "Chancellor Graham of The World Federation of Nations has petitioned this Court to hear the case against Dr. Annette Lynn Deberry and Dr. Anatol Ayala, leaders of an organization known as The Liberty Bell, on the basis that the organization is international in scope and therefore should be adjudicated in The World Federation of Nations' Supreme Court.

"Mr. Thompson, WFN Attorney General, are you ready to represent the chancellor's office?"

Thompson stands to address the Court. "Yes, Your Honors, I am ready with my opening statement." I work hard to pay attention, but my eyes won't leave Mom, who is so still and quiet.

"If it pleases the Court, I will give just a quick statement and get straight to the point because I'm sure you have already read our briefs, which are in the video paper outlining the charges set forth.

"Dr. Annette Deberry and Dr. Anatol Ayala as well as other leaders of the treasonous organization known as The Liberty Bell Movement want to free clones and make cyborgs equal to Firsts. We have proof that they have engaged in a reckless biological experiment that undermines our laws and values. Due to the nature of their crime, they should be handed over to the WFN authorities to stand trial in its Supreme Court.

"Furthermore," Attorney General Thompson drags out his commentary, "we have classified evidence showing that The Liberty Bell Movement is involved in a worldwide conspiracy involving aliens who want to destroy our civilization. The Liberty Bell made first contact with aliens but did not obey the law and alert the authorities."

Justice Michaels, seated at the end, speaks up. "None of the defendants' Miranda rights or civil liberties has been violated nor have the defendants been mistreated in any way. Correct?"

"That is correct," Mr. Thompson confirms.

Justice Alexander Filmore, who is seated to the right of Justice Michaels, interjects. "I see you administered truth serum and mind probes to get information from the defendants. They were in legal amounts?"

"They were. There should be no brain damage due to their use. As you know, Justice Filmore, the extension of the Patriot Act of 2015, passed by the United States Congress, allows police agencies to use any means necessary in all cases dealing with terrorists. As of June 2170, The Liberty Bell Movement has been listed as a terrorist organization and all members as traitors by the chancellor's Executive Order 91289."

Chief Justice Granbury listens carefully but never takes his eyes off me. I work hard not to fidget. I turn my eyes to the

American flags on each side of the bench and feel Granbury's eyes on me. *Is my wig lopsided? Do I have an eyebrow hanging funny?* I feel like a specimen.

Justice Granbury calls for our lawyer, Mr. Adams, to give his opening statement.

Our attorney stands. "We intend to prove that the defendants are innocent of all charges" is the only thing he says before sitting.

"Is that all?" I blurt.

Justice Granbury turns a stern stare on me. "Mute her sound," he says.

Justice Allison comments. "Mr. Adams, the charges against your clients are well documented and all seems to be in order. Why shouldn't we find them guilty and turn them over to The WFN?"

Mr. Adams approaches the bench while Mr. Thompson adjusts himself in his seat. "Your Honor, it is true that my clients are part of The Liberty Bell Movement, a nonviolent group dedicated to the freedom of all oppressed people. As I'm sure you know, The Liberty Bell Movement was started by one of our esteemed Founding Fathers, Benjamin Franklin. Now we are expected to believe that he did so to conspire with aliens to take over the world."

A justice, whose nameplate I can't see, clears his throat and mumbles something about Franklin being a womanizer. Chief Justice Granbury raises his gavel. *Bam!* Down it comes with a sturdy knock. "That was uncalled for."

Mr. Adams goes on. "The defendants have not harmed anyone or destroyed any property. History shows that their work has always been to better humans' relationships with one another."

"Why all the secrecy?" asks Justice Filmore.

Mr. Adams responds quickly. "Are my defendants on trial for belonging to an organization that has its own secrets? If that is the case, the Freemasons, the Elks, Greek sororities and fraternities should be hauled into court and accused of treason. Secrecy is not illegal."

"It is if you're plotting with aliens to overthrow our civilization," says Justice Filmore.

Mr. Adams is scoring, and that's so frisk!

He says, "Let anyone who has proof that The Liberty Bell is conspiring with aliens come forward with evidence — something more than a graphic novel. Otherwise, this Court should throw out the charge of treason against my clients.

"The Liberty Bell Movement wants to make freedom a reality for all human beings, as well as for clones and cyborgs."

"Absolute nonsense," says Justice Kirby, leaping to his feet. "The operative words here are *human beings*. Clones aren't people, and cyborgs are only three-fifths human. They are happiest when they are with their own kind."

Justice Kirby's comment raises a stir of voices in the courtroom.

Chief Justice Granbury's hammering gavel drowns them out. "Outbursts will not be tolerated in this courtroom," he shouts, his face red with emotion. "The next person who shouts — justice or not — will be removed. Do I make myself clear? Chief Marshal, stand ready."

Mr. Adams keeps going. "This Court, the Constitution, the

Congress, the president, the world courts, and The World Federation of Nations have made it very clear that all persons are born free. Clones and cyborgs have been dehumanized by design and law.

"My clients are guilty of compassion but not treason. They are speaking out for those who can't speak for themselves. Clones have the right to life, liberty, and the pursuit of happiness, the same as anyone else. And we have made them slaves, which is in violation of the Thirteenth Amendment to the Constitution of the United States."

Chief Justice Granbury asks, "What do you have to say about this, Attorney General?"

"It is true the Thirteenth Amendment outlaws slavery in the United States. But clones are not slaves, they are biological machines," Attorney General Thompson explains. "*Diamond v. Chakrabarty* in 1980 clearly states that people and companies can own biological machines even though the machine is a living organism. Clones are nothing more than biological mechanisms. Clones are not born but manufactured. They cannot reproduce themselves, and like all machines, they wear out or become obsolete and must be decommissioned.

"More important," he continues, "the Supreme Court ruled in the *Dred Scott v. Sandford* case of 1857 that the Court does not have the authority to make a piece of property a citizen of the United States and grant to that property all the rights citizens have. This means you cannot make a chair or a sewing machine a citizen and allow it to sue its owners. We all know slavery was wrong, but the Court was right when it said a piece of property cannot sue its owners.

"To paraphrase Chief Justice Roger B. Taney's opinion in the Scott case, clones and cyborgs have no rights any human being is bound to honor. Bottom line — the slaves in the eighteenth and nineteenth centuries were humans, not like clones and cyborgs."

The attorney general expresses his argument well, but I don't agree with a word he has said. I wonder if The O are watching any of this. I understand now what they were talking about. Three centuries after slavery, and we're still arguing the same issues. Each side is sure it's right. Will it take another war this time?

Mr. Adams's rebuttal begins with him talking about me. "This is evidence to the contrary," he says, leaning over to my screen image.

"Leanna was *created* by Dr. Ayala, but she is thirteen years old. Clones are supposed to live only twelve years from date of production. Yet Leanna is like any other teenager. She's growing up with a loving mother who gave her a solid upbringing. In fact, Leanna never knew she was a clone until recently."

The whole courtroom breaks into an uproar.

"An abomination!" a woman calls out. The chief marshal escorts her out. It takes a few moments to restore order.

When it's quiet again, Mr. Adams continues. "There is more," he says. "Leanna has a mind of her own. Just ask her mother about that. This girl is proof that clones are not machines. She is a person, and my clients are guilty only of protecting and loving a human being who happens to have second-generation cells. That alone should not negate one's humanity. We have the sworn testimony of twenty-five esteemed doctors who will testify that second-generation cells are not inferior to first.

"Was Frederick Douglass a criminal for choosing freedom? Was Abraham Lincoln a terrorist for issuing the Emancipation Proclamation? *What is the crime here?*"

Justice Kirby rises sharply, but he checks himself before speaking. "You have sunk your own ship. We all know it is a violation of patent law to make biological clones without permission from the Topas Corporation. Any way you spin it, your clients are guilty of breaking a host of clone laws for unlawful purposes. This clone," he says, pointing at me, "should be decommissioned immediately and the defendants turned over to the WFN authorities. This case is outside US jurisdiction."

That's when Chief Justice Granbury turns on my mic and says to me, "Leanna, do you understand what's going on here?"

"Yes. I understand that my mom has been arrested because she wants people to be free. How is that a crime?"

It is so quiet in the courtroom now.

Chief Justice Granbury asks, "Do you really attend school?"

"Yes, I attend the AVS School of Missouri. I love it."

Justice Jackson speaks up for the first time. "What is your favorite class?"

"History is the best. We have virtual field trips to places such as Egypt, China, and the American West. It's really fun. We've even fought in the Civil War, at the Battle of Gettysburg, which was scary but frisk."

The chief justice's piercing gray eyes stay on mine. "Your mother and Dr. Ayala are pleading not guilty on the grounds that the organization to which they belong has not done anything wrong." I can't tell if he is angry or concerned. "Their defense is that even though you are a clone, you are a sentient being and capable of self-determination. Do you know what sentient and self-determination mean?"

"Sentient means I can feel emotions. And of course I know what self-determination is," I say. Stifled laughter comes from somewhere in the room. I am not trying to be funny, just honest.

"We must find out if the defendants' assertions are true," says Justice Kirby. "If you are a sentient being, then of course you would be protected by the Thirteenth and Fourteenth Amendments to the United States Constitution. But how do we know you are a clone? If we can't test you to ascertain the status of your cells, we can't accept you as evidence."

"Tell us where you are staying," says Justice Blakemore, speaking to me on the screen.

Lyle Adams's voice snaps ahead. "You don't have to answer that question, Leanna."

This enrages Justice Blakemore. "Mr. Adams, haven't you been listening? This clone has no rights. She's a biological machine."

Justice Blakemore tries again. "I order you to tell me where you are — now!"

Mom looks frightened but firm. "*No,*" she says simply. Then, louder, "Don't hurt my daughter. You're blinded by bigotry. You see what you want to see."

"Mom!" I scream. But someone has turned down the volume on my virtual.

The chief justice shouts to the marshal, "Get Deberry out of here — shut her up!"

There is a long, uncertain pause.

After several minutes, Chief Justice Granbury addresses me.

"Listen carefully, Leanna," he says. "We are going to decide whether your mother's case goes to the WFN Supreme Court or if the case remains here under our jurisdiction. Right now I don't have much to work with. If you turn yourself in, I can guarantee you will be safe, that nobody will harm you. But if you don't come in and let us run tests to prove your clone status, then it may not go well for your mother and Dr. Ayala."

As he is talking, I notice two things. Behind Chief Justice Granbury is a picture of Justice John Marshall Harlan, one of the Custodians of The Liberty Bell Movement. Chief Justice Granbury has positioned himself under the portrait.

Is this a coincidence?

Then I notice the small American flag pinned to the justice's robe. I have to squint to make sure I am seeing it right. The flag is upside down, which is a sign of distress. Is it possible that the chief justice is a member of The Liberty Bell

Movement and is telling me this by wearing the flag upside down and sitting under Justice Harlan's portrait? Or is this a trick to make me think he is a friend, to gain my trust? I have no way of knowing for sure. I must play it safe.

"I ask again, Leanna, would you voluntarily come in for testing?"

"No," I say. "I won't come in."

Chief Justice Granbury sits back in his chair. He sighs deeply. "Then I have no choice but to turn this case over to the WFN court."

There is a fluttering of loud whispers. "Order!" snaps the chief justice. "I realize this is a highly charged case, but we must maintain order in this courtroom!" He bangs his gavel until everyone is silent.

Chief Justice Granbury speaks to Attorney General Thompson. "One of my responsibilities is to present cases before the World Federation Supreme Court. So I will be seeing you there."

"We'd welcome you to be a part of our team, sir," says Mr. Thompson.

Mr. Adams asks permission to make a motion.

"There is no cause for the defendants to be held in custody under tight security. I recommend that Drs. Deberry and Ayala be released. They offer no flight risk. They welcome taking their case before the world."

"I object," says Justice Kirby.

Then Chief Justice Granbury does the unexpected. "Can we agree to hold them under house arrest with locator chips until their trial?"

A majority of the justices agree.

"So orders this Court, Chief Justice Granbury presiding." He raises his gavel, then strikes it hard.

"All rise," says the chief marshal.

The justices leave the room. The Court evaporates.

When I exit virtual and take off the commglasses, I know something is wrong. Zion is pacing. Houston looks worried.

"Leanna," Zion says, "I don't know how, and I'm not sure, but I think you've been traced."

"I thought these were untraceables."

Zion shrugs. "They're supposed to be."

Houston says, "The indicators show that while you were in virtual, there was a power surge that could be caused by a number of things, including a trace. We can't take any chances. We need to move you to another station."

Zion explains that a farcar will be waiting for us at the south fly-out in twenty minutes. If we aren't there, the driver will leave. "And you'll be on your own. So get there!" Zion tells us.

"Okay," I say, taking off my wig and reaching for the jar of purple stage makeup.

With my disguise in place, I pad along behind Houston, who has helped me get my backpack up onto both shoulders. As we hurry to the elevator, he says, "I'm ready to sign on with The Liberty Bell Movement. What do I do?"

"Well, I've been told you'll know what to do when your time comes. It's like taking a bite out of an elephant."

"What?"

"I'll explain later."

The elevator doors open, and there is Joe Spiller and his two nasty biobots! It takes Spiller a moment to recognize me in my disguise.

"You!" he growls.

Houston pushes me out of the way as the first biobot springs out of the elevator into the hallway. It opens its large mouth to attack like a dog.

Spiller, who is still in the elevator, orders the second biobot to "eliminate the defective clone after taking out this Metal Head!"

The automatic doors to the elevator won't close. Biobot #1 bounces toward Houston with its razor-sharp teeth. It bites into Houston's arm, sending him to the floor in pain. Everything is happening so fast. I'm frozen, but only for a second. I snap into motion once I see biobot #2 also advancing toward Houston.

Houston can survive a biobot bite, but for me it would be fatal. Figuring it's best for me to keep moving, I use one of my best swifting moves — a backward handspring that lets me land a kick to the biobot.

"Good one," shouts Houston.

The first biobot wastes no time moving in.

Houston waits until the thing tries to bite him again. When the biobot approaches, he gives it a bionic kick, sending it sliding down the hallway.

Spiller snatches both my arms from behind and drags me onto the elevator.

I stomp on his foot as hard as I can. Spiller's grip loosens just enough for me to yank myself away.

Houston tries to grab Spiller, but Spiller's too quick. He catches Houston's ankle and shoves him down the hallway.

Spiller pushes me against the wall and heads toward Houston. "I don't need bionic parts to be stronger and better than you, Metal Head." He spits at Houston. This fight is no longer business for Spiller. It's now personal. He wants to match his brute strength against Houston's bionic enhancements.

"Let's get animated!" says Houston, taunting Spiller.

"Want we should get him, boss?" asks one of the biobots. The two of them are functional again.

"Stand down," Spiller orders. "This one is mine."

Houston can take out Spiller in a fair match, but Spiller doesn't know the meaning of fair.

Spiller reaches inside his boot and pulls out a laser tube he's sneaked past security. A laser shot can't deliver a fatal wound, but it can disable Houston long enough to give Spiller the advantage.

In my pocket is a small bottle of purple face paint to use as a touch-up for my clone disguise. I run straight at Spiller, screaming, and he falls for my trick by tossing me aside. As I fall to the floor, I throw the purple paint in his face.

He drops the laser tube as he shields his eyes. He calls on his biobots for help. "Get 'em!"

Before the biobots can respond, Houston scoops up the laser tube and we head for the steps.

"The biobots' weapons were deactivated when they entered Atlantis," says Houston as we run. "The tube won't stop them, but it might slow them down."

Houston turns back and fires into the mouth of an advancing biobot.

Taking the stairs two at a time, down four flights, we get to the bottom and race out of the building into the street.

We can hear Spiller and the biobots behind us.

Houston ducks into a small wooded area. "We're going to have to fight. Which one do you want, Spiller or his biobots?"

"I'll hold off Spiller for as long as I can," I say.

"Use his weight against him."

"Okay, Houston. Once you get the biobots, come help me. Let's do this."

Spiller and the hounds are in the woods with us.

"Hey you, Paint Face!" Houston taunts Spiller.

"This way," Spiller says, "We've got 'em now."

"No you don't," I say, jumping from behind a tree and giving Spiller a knee to the groin. He bends quickly. I snatch his commglasses and hurl them as far away as I can, so he is not able to call for help.

The biobots are crouched and ready to spring on Houston. He uses his bionic arm to grab them by their antennae. In a single fluid motion, Houston tosses those ugly things over a small embankment. "That's from my uncle Li Rizin," he calls to Spiller.

Spiller is still bent from the pain in his groin. Houston and I strap him to a tree with his own belt and shirt.

He swears at us and promises revenge. "Li Rizin? I should have known he was involved in all this," he says, spitting. "You tell him for me that he's in over his head. You'd better give up now."

"What, and miss all the fun?" Houston is giddy now.

But the biobots spring up on the path. Houston turns quickly and fires at them with the laser tube. They crash down the embankment again, howling and wailing.

"You're mine!" Spiller yells, already working to free himself.

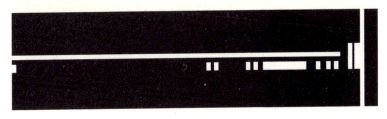

We run two blocks when we realize we've missed our farcar fly-out. We're trapped.

"Let's go this way," Houston says, heading back to Holmiester.

"Hold up," I say, catching my breath. "I have an idea. Follow me."

We reach the hangar and slip through a side entrance. "RUBy," I call. "It's us. Houston and #1010."

The doors open and we quickly run on board.

"Security reports that there is a *savage cyborg* and a *defective clone* that are being sought. Would you know anything about that?" Carlos asks.

Houston doesn't have to wonder if he should tell him the truth. "It's us," he says. "And we need to get out of here now."

RUBy's engines fire up. "I'm heading for Mars," she says. "Get off, Carlos."

"Could you drop us off on the Moon?" Houston negotiates with the computer. But RUBy only seems to be interested in Carlos.

"Get off, Carlos," RUBy says more forcefully.

"No, no. I'm staying. Please."

Obviously, we are in the middle of something we don't understand. We move to the side and listen.

The doors open. RUBy repeats the order. "Go. Now." Carlos refuses to leave.

"Okay, this is it," he says. "I have the code that opens the dome fly-out. I won't give it to you unless you include me."

"Who's in charge here, the computer or you?" Houston asks Carlos.

RUBy and Carlos answer at the same time, "I'm in charge."

A security team comes storming through. Zion is there, pretending to be part of security. Spiller follows with the damaged biobots, along with a man who identifies himself as Dr. Marcus Pace.

"Get off that ship," orders Zion, who is playing his role well. If we hadn't known better, we would have thought he was one of them.

"Boy! I want you and those people off that ship immediately," shouts Dr. Pace.

Carlos pulls his shoulders back. "Sorry, Dad. I can't. I've got to go with RUBy."

"Son, you have no idea what you're doing. Those people you are with are wanted criminals. Shut RUBy down now."

Dr. Pace doesn't get it. Carlos can't shut RUBy down. She's acting on her own.

Dr. Pace is frustrated. "Let my son off," he calls to me and Houston. "Don't add kidnapping to your list of crimes."

Carlos keys in a code. He tells us to take our seats and belt up. There's a thud, and the roof of the hangar slides back with a single snap. Above us the fly-out opens. I make eye contact with Zion. I see a hint of a smile. I smile back — the best thank-you I can give him.

Dr. Pace runs to the control panel along the wall. RUBy has locked them out. No way to stop us. "If you hurt my son, I'll see to it that you never see a free day again!" shouts Dr. Pace.

"I'm a cyborg," Houston shouts. "I have no freedom."

Just then, as if released from a huge slingshot, the ship projects upward in a spinning spiral through the fly-out and into Earth's atmosphere.

As we climb, RUBy blasts her secondary jets and releases us from the planet's gravitational pull.

From my seat in the command center, I see Earth as a big blue-green marble grow smaller. The first thing I'm going to do when I reach the Moon is call Mom. I have so much to tell her, especially about being visited by The O. Then I'll contact Sandra and see what happens, good or bad. Will we ever be able to go fringing again?

RUBy's screen flashes yellow. She is at work. They are not rocks, The O said. What are they, then? What am I supposed to do? I wonder about my future and what will be demanded of me. But for now, I close my eyes and let the light of RUBy's screen wash over me as I drift off to sleep.

A HISTORY OF THE FUTURE

This novel is a work of futuristic fiction based on historical events.

Like The O depicted in the book, spherical time is used to observe the past, present, and future simultaneously. After researching and writing several works about American slavery, we were inspired to write *The Clone Codes*. Set in the year 2170, Leanna's virtual journal entries tell the story of the ongoing struggle for freedom and justice led by The Liberty Bell Movement.

Supreme Court decisions, morality, and cloning are current issues that helped us construct *The Clone Codes*. Here are the facts and the fiction that weave a history of the future.

FACT: For three and half centuries, Africa provided Europe and the New World with an endless supply of cheap labor. Slaveholders dehumanized Africans by describing them as inferior, deceptive beings who were lazy and immoral. These stereotypes lasted for many years after slavery ended, making it impossible for African Americans to share in the benefits of equal citizenship.

FICTION: *The Clone Codes* is about a slavocracy set in the future. Clones are manufactured biological beings designed to work and serve their owners. They are not considered sentient, which means they have no emotions. They are called by the pejorative "Seconds" because of their second-generation cell structure.

FACT: The Fugitive Slave Act of 1850 made it a federal crime for anyone to help runaway slaves. "Slave catchers" tracked down runaways and returned them to their masters for a price.

FICTION: In the future, these bounty hunters became the Clone Humane Society.

FACT: Fear of punishment didn't stop slaves from running, and it didn't stop people from helping them. The Underground Railroad was a secret escape route with safe houses along the way called "stations," operated by ordinary people known as "conductors." These abolitionists were considered criminal, and if caught, were imprisoned or fined.

FICTION: The Liberty Bell Movement is modeled after the nineteenth-century abolitionists who defied the law in order to change the system.

FACT: The United States Constitution considered slaves to be three-fifths of a person.

FICTION: In the future, the same language discriminates against cyborgs. Three of their five major internal or external organs have been replaced with artificial "enhancers." Because cyborgs are physically enhanced, they are given the most dangerous jobs under the most difficult circumstances and are forced to live in segregated neighborhoods and go to segregated schools.

FACT: The Thirteenth Amendment to the US Constitution ended slavery. As a result, slavery was prohibited in the United States. But in 1980, the Supreme Court ruled in the *Diamond v. Chakrabarty* case that "living organisms" can be patented or "owned."

FICTION: In the future, the *Diamond v. Chakrabarty* case opened the door for the fictionalized Topas Corporation to mass-produce, own, and sell clones, whom they define as "living organisms."

FACT: As far back as colonial times, slaveholders passed laws known as the Slave Codes to control slaves and stop rebellions. These laws differed from colony to colony, and later state to state, but most of them forbade slaves to hold meetings unless a master was present. Slaves were required to have legal passes when away from their plantation. Slaves couldn't own a weapon, enter into a contract, buy property, vote, testify against a white person, or strike a white person, even in self-defense. The most troubling code stipulated that slaves couldn't be taught to read or write. It was illegal to teach them. Following the Civil War, the former states of the Confederacy passed Black Codes, which were intended to restrict the freedom of emancipated slaves. Many of the Black Codes became state and federal laws, referred to by some as Jim Crow, until they were found to be unconstitutional during the Civil Rights movement of the 1960s.

FICTION: In the future, the Black Codes become the Clone Codes.

THE CUSTODIANS:

In *The Clone Codes*, The O visit four people from the past in order to change the future. Three are historical heroes. One is a fictional character.

FACT: The three historical figures are:

BENJAMIN FRANKLIN (1706-1790)

The O chose Benjamin Franklin to be a Custodian because he was a revolutionary leader, writer, scientist, philosopher, framer of the United States Constitution, and statesman. Franklin was born in Boston, but later moved to Philadelphia, living among the Quakers, who began the abolitionist movement. Some people think the US Constitution is a perfect document. Franklin knew better, and that's why he fought hard to make the document amendable. Through the years, the US Constitution has changed to meet the needs of the people and has evolved into a universal icon of freedom.

JUSTICE JOHN MARSHALL HARLAN (1833-1911)

On May 18, 1896, the US Supreme Court ruled that it was constitutional for the government to maintain separate public facilities for black and white citizens if the facilities were equal. Justice John Marshall Harlan, from a Kentucky slaveholding family, strongly opposed his colleagues' decision. "Our Constitution is color-blind," he wrote, "and neither knows nor tolerates classes among citizens." Harlan predicted that the *Plessy v. Ferguson* case, like the Dred Scott decision of 1857, would "arouse race hate." The O chose Justice Harlan because he would have understood the legal arguments regarding citizenship.

ELEANOR ROOSEVELT (1884-1962)

First Lady Eleanor Roosevelt was the wife of President Franklin D. Roosevelt, who was elected for an unprecedented four terms and served in office from 1933 to 1945. The Roosevelts shepherded the country through the difficult years of the Great Depression and World War II. Mrs. Roosevelt was known and respected for her work on behalf of women and minorities. After her husband's death, she continued his work by helping organize the United Nations, a predecessor of the futuristic organization in *The Clone Codes* known as The World Federation of Nations.

FICTION: Here is a brief bio of our fictional Custodian, Dr. David H. Montgomery.

DR. DAVID H. MONTGOMERY (2057-2142)

In 2089, a human baby was cloned, making it possible for infertile couples to have children. Thousands of them were created. Most were healthy and happy, until the first clone children reached age twelve. Suddenly, at the onset of puberty, their cells burned out and corrupted, and they died. Families were devastated. Nations passed laws that stopped all infant cloning.

Montgomery was a Nobel Prize-winning physician and engineer, who in 2102 found a method to create adult clones who could help populate the newly constructed Moon colony. The Topas Corporation bought his patent and began producing adult clones as servants, who were enslaved by their "Firsts." Dr. Montgomery was horrified when he saw how the Topas Corporation had used his work. He dedicated his life to the struggle to free clones, secure their legal rights, and establish their humanity.

TRUTHS.

LIES.

HISTORY.

RULES.

THE FUTURE.

MORE . . .

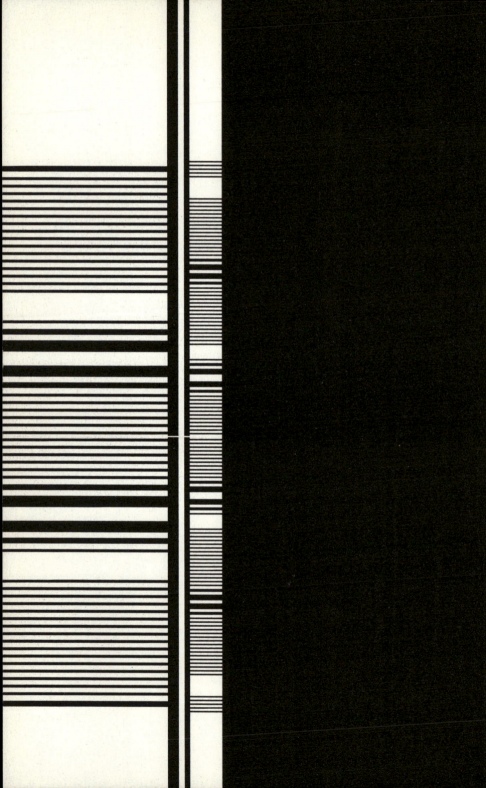

n Leanna's world, so much is determined by laws and by the authority of the governing bodies that use these regulations o oppress. As the Clone Codes trilogy unfolds, even more is revealed about pasts that never seem to end – and futures hat are infinite.

Like swifting, you can't play the game if you don't know the rules of this strange and powerful universe.

n the next Clone Codes installment, Houston, a cyborg, tells his story. Here are the rules of Houston's universe.

What Is a Cyborg?

By order of The World Federation of Nations (WFN), as of January 1, 2084, all persons who have been enhanced with three or more biofe, or synthetic body or organ replacements, shall be classified as three-fifths of a human being, or a cyborg.

The Cyborg Act of 2130

For the security and general welfare of the cyborg race, these protections have been established on this 7th Day of October, 2130.

John P. Haversham
Director of the Bureau of Cyborg Affairs

THE CYBORG CODES

■ All cyborgs must be registered with the Bureau of Cyborg Affairs (BCA).

■ Those that are cyborgs must live within designated areas set aside on the Moon Colony. If a cyborg desires to live or work elsewhere, it must acquire BCA permission.

■ It is mandated that cyborgs may not serve as officers in the World Federation of Nations' defense forces or serve in any national law enforcement agencies.

■ Cyborg children must attend one of four cyborg academies based on test scores and abilities.

■ All cyborgs over the age of 16 must be employed.

■ Cyborgs need permission from the BCA to marry or have children.

■ The BCA will provide cyborgs with medical insurance and health-care needs.

■ Cyborgs cannot inherit real property.

■ Cyborgs can only participate in amateur or professional sports within the Cyborg Leagues.

ABOUT THE AUTHORS

Newbery Honor winner Patricia C. McKissack has collaborated on many critically acclaimed books with her husband, Fredrick L. McKissack. Together, they are the authors of numerous award winners, including *Rebels Against Slavery: American Slave Revolts* and *Black Hand, White Sails: The Story of African American Whalers*, both Coretta Scott King Honor Books, and *Sojourner Truth: Ain't I a Woman?* a Coretta Scott King Honor Book and winner of the *Boston Globe*/Horn Book Award. Patricia and Fredrick McKissack live in St. Louis, Missouri.

John McKissack, the son of Patricia and Fredrick, is a licensed mechanical engineer. *The Clone Codes* marks his debut as a writer. John is married to Michelle McKissack, and they are the parents of three sons, Peter, James Everett, and John. He resides in Memphis, Tennessee.

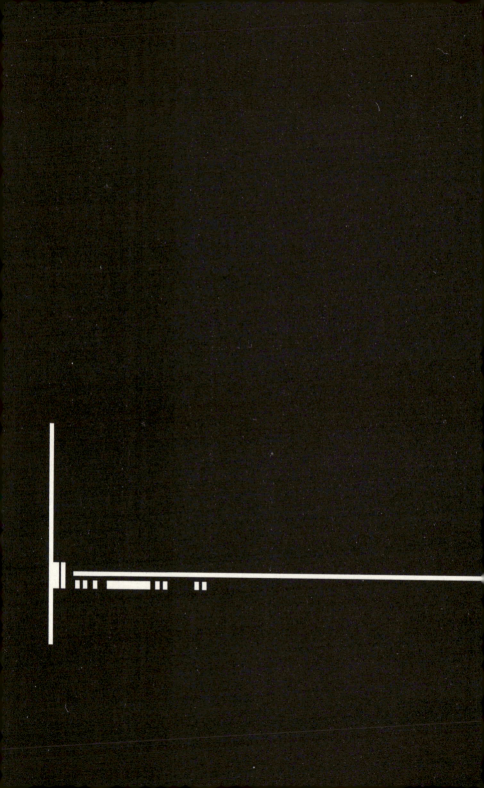

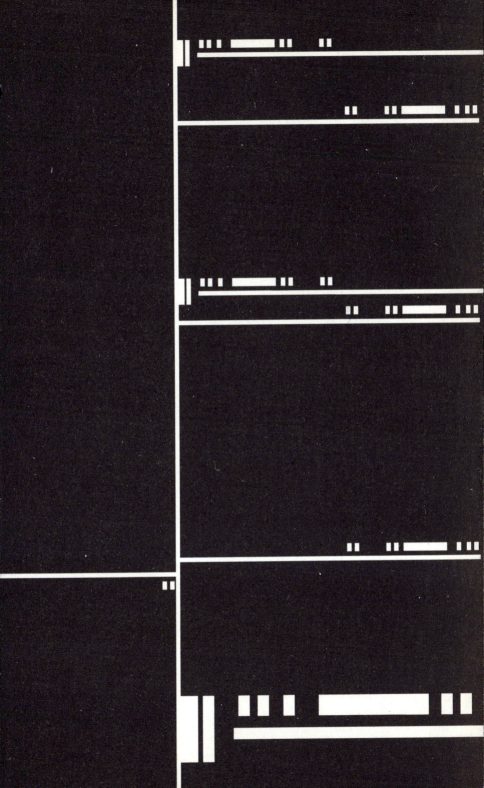

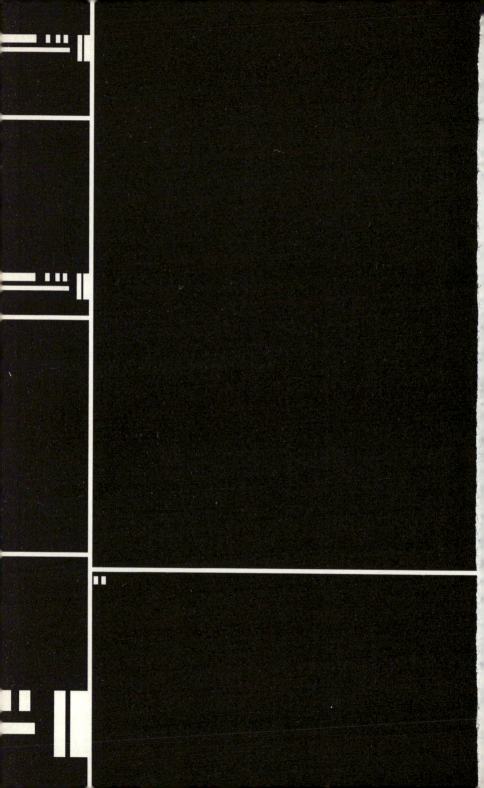